Crescat

B064

FACE FROM THE PAST

When handsome Dr Julian Ransome re-enters her life so many years after their relationship ended, midwife Maudie Rouse isn't sure how to react. But nothing about her old flame is as it seems, and she begins to suspect that something is very wrong. What has happened to the man she once knew? When danger threatens, can she survive it to marry her new love?

CATRIONA McCUAIG

---◆---

FACE FROM THE PAST

A Midwife Maudie Rouse mystery

Complete and Unabridged

LINFORD
Leicester

First published in Great Britain in 2013

First Linford Edition
published 2015

A catalogue record for this book is available
from the British Library.

ISBN 978–1–4448–2411–7

Published by
F. A. Thorpe (Publishing)
Anstey, Leicestershire

Set by Words & Graphics Ltd.
Anstey, Leicestershire
Printed and bound in Great Britain by
T. J. International Ltd., Padstow, Cornwall

This book is printed on acid-free paper

1

'Here we are again!' Dick Bryant raised his glass to his fiancée, Maudie Rouse. 'Our second Christmas together. It seems like no time at all since we were sitting here last Christmas. This year has gone by in a flash.'

'It certainly has,' Maudie agreed. 'That's because so much has happened.' She got up to put more coal on the fire, musing over all that had taken place in her small world. For a start, she had been kept busy ushering new babies into the world. In and around Llandyfan, her small English village on the border with South Wales, there had been a real boom in new arrivals since the war had ended four years ago. Serving men and women had returned to their families to take up civilian life again. The people of Britain looked forward to an existence in which their children could expect to grow up without bombs falling out of the night-time sky. Many items were still rationed, or in short supply, and the availability of new housing had not yet caught up with the demand — but everyone was aware of better times coming, just around the corner.

Meanwhile, Maudie was looking forward to her wedding, which was supposed to take place in June or July. She might have been married by now but for the fact that Constable Dick Bryant had gone to Canada on an exchange programme having to do with rural policing. He had suggested they get married before he left so that Maudie could accompany him, but she had declined. To begin with she was under contract as the local midwife, and she wanted to see her expectant mums through to term. And if she had gone to Canada, what was she supposed to do in a strange country while her husband was carrying out his duties there?

'Are we going to open our presents now?' Dick asked, his eyes wide open in anticipation as he settled into an armchair by the fire. Maudie smiled. He looked just like a little boy hoping for a new train set. She only hoped he wouldn't be disappointed by the socks she'd knitted him. Men were so difficult to buy for! She didn't know his taste in ties, and although she'd searched the shops for inspiration, nothing had come to mind.

'Open mine first,' he said, passing her a flat package that felt surprisingly heavy. 'Mind you don't drop it; it might break. I had a job keeping it in one piece getting it home from Canada.'

Intrigued, she carefully removed the outer wrapping, smoothing out the holly-patterned paper to put away for future use. She opened the white box to reveal a decorative plate nestled in a bed of tissue paper.

'Do you like it, Maudie? Do you see? It shows the Dionne quintuplets when they were babies. It made me think of you, being a midwife.'

'It's lovely, Dick. Thank you very much.' Fascinated, she stared at the china image of the five identical little girls, each one propped up in a high chair of her own. Of course she knew who the

Dionnes were. Could there be anyone in the civilised world who hadn't heard of them? At the time of their birth, and at regular intervals ever since, all the newspapers and magazines had been full of the event. Born two months prematurely in a remote farmhouse in Ontario, the babies had weighed less than fourteen pounds in all. The birth of quintuplets had been described as a miracle. For Maudie, the miracle was that they had all survived. She was well aware that it was touch and go for a seventh-month baby to survive at all; the Dionne story boggled the mind.

'Of course they are not babies any-more,' Dick observed. 'They must be fourteen years old by now. I found that plate in a sort of second-hand-cum-souvenir shop. They had all sorts of Dionne items. Everything from teaspoons to colouring books for kiddies showing the little girls.'

'Fancy.'

'I did think of going to that Corbeil place where they were born. You used to be able to get a look at the little girls, but

I understand they don't display them to the public anymore.'

'I should think not!' Maudie said. She was interested in the quins as much as anyone else — perhaps more, given her occupation — but the idea of children being paraded behind wire netting like animals in a zoo revolted her. Still, others felt differently, and could more than three million people be wrong? That was said to be the number of people who had visited the specially built hospital where the girls had lived. Even the king and queen had gone to see the sisters during an official visit to Canada.

Dick interrupted these musings. 'Come on, then old girl! Don't you have a present for me?'

'Of course.' Maudie reached into her knitting bag and handed him a bulky parcel containing two pairs of socks.

He looked at them appreciatively, smoothing them with one calloused hand. 'These black ones will do fine with my uniform this coming winter. My feet get so cold in those thin things I have at home, and they're all lumpy with darns.'

'And the brown ones will go with those off duty shoes of yours. I was lucky to find enough wool for those in that little draper's in Midvale.'

As for the black ones, she had carefully unpicked an old jumper of her own and washed and wound the wool before knitting it up again, but she wasn't going to tell him that!

'I'll try out these brown ones right away,' Dick said, reaching down to remove his brown oxfords.

'Not at the table!' Maudie shrieked. Dick looked her in surprise.

'We're not at the table now,' he said.

'No, but the remains of the pudding are still there. I'd better go and put it away.' She jumped to her feet, stopped by Dick's restraining hand.

'If we're going to be wed you'll have to learn not to faint at the sight of a man's bare foot, Maudie Rouse.'

'I've seen plenty of bare feet, and worse, thank you very much. I haven't always been a midwife, you know. I've looked after plenty of men in my time.'

'Never mind all that. There's something

I have to tell you.'

'That sounds ominous. I hope it's not going to be a repeat of last Christmas, when you told me you were off to Canada for six months.'

Dick settled back in his chair, obviously trying to find the right words for what he had to say. Maudie felt a sudden surge of love for this teddy bear of a man, sitting there with one shoe off and a paper hat on his head. She waited for him to speak.

'Well,' he said at last, 'it seems that the powers that be are pleased with what I did in Canada.'

'And so they should be,' Maudie said. Disregarding his own safety, Dick had nipped into a corral and saved a toddler from a dangerous bull. He had managed to get out before being gored, but in hurling himself over the fence he had landed awkwardly and broken an arm.

'Oh, it wasn't just the bull thing. They seemed to think I did quite well at representing British policing over there.'

'Of course you did.'

'Anyway, now I've been given the chance to switch to the detective side.'

'But you've been studying for your sergeant's exams.'

'That's right, but ever since I was a little boy I've wanted to be a detective, and I must say that the idea of being Detective Sergeant Dick Bryant has a certain appeal.'

'I don't know if we could stand having two detectives in the family,' Maudie said, laughing. The truth was that she rather fancied herself as a sort of modern Miss Marple, and why not? Was it her fault that murder seemed to follow her around?

Dick seemed to accept this in the spirit in which it was said, smiling indulgently in return. 'So what do you think, Maudie?'

'Well of course, if that's that you want to do, Dick, you must follow your dream. When does your promotion take effect?'

'Whoa, back! It's by no means certain. To even be considered I shall have to take further training. It means taking courses at the Police College at Hendon.'

'Hendon!'

'Yes, in Middlesex. Near London.'

'Middlesex.' Aware that she was beginning to sound like an echo, Maudie bit her lip.

'Come on, then. Tell me what you think.'

'It means I won't see you for weeks on end,' she blurted. 'It's too far away, Dick.'

'It's not as bad as all that, love. I'll be able to come back at weekends.'

'Not if you're meant to be studying what they've taught you through the week.'

Dick reached up and pulled off his blue paper hat, crumpling it in his hand. 'Well, you know the answer to that one, Maudie. Marry me and come with me.'

'Oh, not again, Dick! You suggested that before you went off to Canada, and you know what my answer was then.'

'This is different. You wouldn't be in a foreign country this time. You could have a wonderful time in London, seeing all the sights. Look, I don't have to give them an answer right away. Please have a think about it, and give me your answer next weekend. If you really don't like the idea of my doing this, then of course I'll forget about it. I love you, Maudie, and I only want you to be happy.'

2

'And that's where we left it,' Maudie said miserably.

Her friend nodded sympathetically. As the wife of the vicar of St John's, Joan Blunt was well used to lending a listening ear to people with problems. 'And you don't want him to go in for this new career; is that it?'

'Of course he should become a detective if that is what he really wants to do, and I know it's my place to be supportive. I know how I'd have felt back in my hospital days if someone had poured cold water on my plan to take midder training. It's just that this is a bit much, coming on top of his going to Canada for all those months.'

'Then perhaps you should go with him to Hendon? As he says, you'll still be in England, and there are all sorts of wonderful things to see and do in London. It could be a lovely long holiday for you.'

'But not the sort of honeymoon I'd envisaged. That sort of thing was all very well during the war when people married in a hurry so they could snatch a few hours together before the husband went off to fight. But I was hoping for a bit more than that. And I still want to get married on a summer morning in St John's, with all my friends around me.'

'And you in a lovely white gown, with orange blossoms in your hair.'

'Hardly that. I'm a bit long in the tooth for that sort of get-up. I was thinking more along the lines of a pretty summer frock and a stunning hat.'

'You could still have that, of course,' Mrs Blunt said. 'Just continue with your original plan of a summer wedding, while encouraging Dick to continue with his training. After all, whatever work he does in the future will benefit both of you. I'm sure that he can get a weekend off to come back to Llandyfan to marry his lady-love.'

Maudie picked at the bobbles on her friend's red chenille tablecloth. 'Oh, why does everything have to be so difficult? I

11

love Dick and I want to be with him, but I wish things didn't have to change!'

'Is there something else, Nurse?'

Maudie sniffed, fumbling in her pocket for a handkerchief. 'He's talking about going back to Canada.'

'What, not another police exchange?'

'No. It's about going for good. Permanently.'

'Good grief! I hope this isn't a case of 'go along with my plans or I'll join the Foreign Legion' or something, is it? I wouldn't have thought that emotional blackmail was Dick's style at all.'

'Not exactly,' Maudie said, her mind going back to their discussion on Christmas night. Dick had leaned forward and taken her hand, looking serious.

'As I said, Maudie, I'll do whatever makes you happy, but I don't want to stay a constable all my life. I'd like to spread my wings a bit, find out what I'm capable of. Can you understand that?'

'Of course I can, and you deserve to be happy, too. You mustn't miss this chance, Dick. I'm sure they don't take just anyone at Hendon. You've earned the privilege.'

'To be honest, love, until this offer came my way I was thinking of taking another course of action entirely.'

'Oh, yes?'

'They told me in Canada that if I'd like to settle there permanently they'd make me very welcome and would do all they could to get me accepted into their ranks. That medal they gave me for saving the little girl carries a bit of weight, I gather, when they're taking on new men.'

'Canada! But wouldn't you have to take their preliminary exams in order to get accepted? Otherwise every Tom, Dick and Harry would try to get into the force.'

'Perhaps I would, but then I'm facing a lot of studying here if I hope for promotion, so what's the difference?'

'You'd have to start again at the bottom,' Maudie warned, but Dick wasn't listening.

'We'll get married this coming summer, as you've wanted, and then we'll go out to Canada, having a lovely honeymoon aboard ship.'

Sick as a donkey all the way, Maudie thought, but she said nothing.

'Hordes of people from all over Europe are doing that right now, and Canada welcomes them all,' Dick went on. 'How about it, Maudie?'

'It's something to think about, certainly.'

'And think about this — you're always grumbling about the fact that married women aren't allowed to work in British hospitals. It's different in Canada. One of my friends over there has a wife who is a nurse, and she told me all about it. They only work eight-hour shifts, you see. Isn't that something?'

It certainly sounded like heaven to Maudie. In the hospital where she'd done her training the staff had gone on duty at seven a.m. and got off at eight p.m., and that was only if all work on the ward was completed by that time of the evening. During those thirteen hours they'd been given three hours off, either from ten to one or from two to five, but it still made for an exhausting day. The best shift lasted from seven to five, but you only received those the day before your day off.

The night shift was something else

again; you worked for twelve hours straight through. Maudie had never forgotten being on duty the night before the clocks were put back and she'd had to endure thirteen hours on the job. To make matters worse, her ward had not been busy that night and the time had dragged on as if it would never end.

'Eight hours!' she marvelled now. It sounded like heaven. What spoiled that lovely thought was the knowledge that she would most likely have to pass exams over there too, and she had almost torn her hair out the first time around, trying to cram facts into her head.

The British S.R.N. was given the best training in the world, but that wasn't enough for countries who wanted to make sure that newcomers met their standards. She had heard that even qualified doctors had to do a year of internship when they first arrived in their chosen country.

She and Dick had stayed up until past midnight discussing the pros and cons. Luckily he had borrowed a motorbike from a pal and didn't have to rush off to catch the last bus, or risk having to hike the twelve miles back to Midvale.

'If I do go to Hendon I'll invest in one of these,' he told Maudie, patting the shining Norton lovingly. 'Then I'll be able to zip back at weekends in no time.'

★ ★ ★

'It sounds to me as if Dick is prepared to give you every chance to decide on a plan you can both be comfortable with,' Mrs Blunt said, giving Maudie a tentative smile. 'It's a rare man who would give a woman that much consideration.'

'I know, I know! It's me that's being unreasonable,' Maudie wailed. 'And if he has to spend the rest of his life working to support the pair of us it should be in a job he finds fulfilling. I'm well aware that not everyone is so lucky.'

'It sounds to me as if you've already decided which way to jump.'

'I think so. Canada is not for me. I'm sure it's a grand country and it would be lovely to travel over there some day and see it all, but to settle there? I'm afraid

I'm not the pioneering type.'

'No, I can't see you crossing the prairie in a covered wagon with your face hidden by a sun bonnet.'

'Now you're taking the mickey! They have skyscrapers in Toronto.'

Mrs Blunt grinned. 'So will you be going to Hendon with Dick?'

Maudie shook her head. 'No, I'll stay here and we'll have the wedding in the summer as planned. After that, much will depend on where Dick gets a job. He's certain to be transferred out of Midvale, I should think. I can't deny that leaving Llandyfan will be an awful wrench after all these years, but there you are. That's life.'

'It might be good for you to go to pastures new where you aren't reminded every day of the murders you've been involved in here. I don't suppose you'll miss those!'

'Being married to a detective won't necessarily protect me from any future involvement,' Maudie told her. 'Besides, I doubt very much if we'll see any more violent crime here. Not in a peaceful village like Llandyfan.'

3

The New Year came in quietly. Dick was on duty on New Year's Eve so there was no chance of the pair of them going out to celebrate.

'It's all hands to the pump,' he told Maudie. 'Not that we're expecting any trouble beyond a few party-goers having one two many and making a nuisance of themselves in the streets. How do you plan to bring in the New Year?'

'I expect I'll just stay in and make a few resolutions that I'll break by the end of next week,' she told him, laughing. It wasn't for him to know that she meant to lose a few pounds before her wedding!

'No babies expected, then?'

'Not for a couple of weeks. I shan't get my face in the *Midvale Chronicle*.'

This was a reference to their weekly newspaper that always made a big thing of the first baby of the year. There was always a photo of the beaming parents with their infant, with possibly the midwife looking over their shoulders as well. Local businesses donated useful items to the family, such as baby supplies, and the lucky recipients received a year's subscription to the newspaper as well.

The first confinement that was pending was for a Mrs Dilys Pugh, a faded blonde with a timid manner. The lady was rather old to be expecting her first child, compared with most of the other mothers in Maudie's care. She admitted to being thirty-five but looked older.

Maudie hadn't taken to the husband at all. Raymond Pugh was an accountant, and one of those men who had to be right about everything. His wife seemed to cope with him by meekly saying 'yes, dear' to all his pronouncements. Shortly before Christmas he had marched his wife into Maudie's cramped little office in the parish hall and demanded that she be given extra-special care, since it had taken her long enough to get in the family way, and he didn't want anything to go wrong. This should have reassured Maudie, but it left her with the impression that Mr

Raymond Pugh would regard anything less than a perfect outcome as a personal affront.

'Rest assured that your wife will receive the best of care, Mr Pugh. Now, I should like to examine Mrs Pugh, so if you wouldn't mind stepping outside, please . . . '

'I prefer to stay,' he said stiffly.

Maudie's eyebrows rose. Most men would run a mile before being subjected to gynaecological details, so why did this chap have to be different?

'That won't be necessary, thank you,' she told him, holding the door open so that he was forced to take the hint and leave. She closed it after him with unnecessary force.

'This baby means a lot to him,' Dilys whispered, as if this excused the man's behaviour.

'I'm sure it does, Mrs Pugh. Now if you hop up on the couch here I'd like to have a look at your tummy.'

Everything seemed to be in order, and Maudie estimated her patient to be seven months along. The Pughs were recent newcomers to the village, but Dilys explained that she had been having proper antenatal care in Leicester, where they'd lived previously.

'Well then, I expect I'll be seeing you early in February,' Maudie said, making a note on the new chart she'd filled out with the pertinent details. 'I'll give you my card. As you'll see, it gives my telephone number here and my home number as well.'

'What if you're not in either place when I need you?' Dilys asked fearfully.

'Then you should call the doctor. Or if all else fails, try the vicar. He can usually think of something.'

The woman looked puzzled. 'You mean he'll pray for help?'

Maudie chuckled. 'No, although I wouldn't put it past him to try that as well! No, what I meant was he always knows what's going on in the village and round about — who I'm likely to be visiting at a given time, for instance — so he can usually track me down.'

'Oh. But what if we have a storm and the telephone lines are out of order? What

21

will we do then?'

Really, the woman was a bundle of nerves, Maudie thought. It was a psychiatrist she needed, not a midwife! 'I'll give you directions to my cottage,' she said. 'It's just around the corner from here. If you need me in a hurry your husband can come and knock on my door, day or night. There is absolutely nothing to worry about.'

She was about to conclude their meeting when a sharp rap came at the door.

'What's going on in there? Are you all right, Dilys?'

Maudie pasted a sweet smile on her face and opened the door. 'All is well, Mr Pugh. You can look forward to greeting a healthy child a couple of months from now.'

He ignored her, addressing his wife in a hectoring tone. 'Come on, then, woman! I haven't got all day!'

'Yes, dear,' Dilys said, sidling past Maudie.

'Thank you, Nurse. Nice meeting you, Nurse,' Maudie muttered as she watched them go. Fortunately most of her patients were very different. Oh, there might be some shouting and cursing while they were actually in labour; that was only to be expected. When it was all over though, and the mother settled with a welcome cup of tea, people were grateful, and even joyful at times. Maudie's efforts were greatly appreciated and people didn't hesitate to tell her so. That made up for the rare awkward customer such as Raymond Pugh.

★　★　★

She was restocking her black bag prior to setting off to make some home visits when the vicar's wife looked in. 'Hello, Nurse. I'm the bearer of bad news, I'm afraid.'

Maudie's jaw dropped. 'Not another murder, I hope!'

'No, no, not that. It's old Doctor Mallory. Harold has just received word that he's passed away.'

'Oh, I'm sorry to hear that. Mind you, he must have been close to ninety. Was he

23

in the cottage hospital?'

'No, at his sister's house. As you know, he went to stay with her when he finally retired. It seems that when she went in with his early-morning cup of tea she found him lying dead in his bed, looking quite peaceful. He must have gone in his sleep.'

'That's a blessing.'

'Yes, indeed. After all he's done for other people over the years he deserved a gentle passing.'

The two women stood in silence for a long moment, contemplating what they knew of the old man. Born in Queen Victoria's reign, he had spent his life working as an old-fashioned country medical practitioner. He had made house calls, delivered babies and occasionally performed operations with the patient laid out on the kitchen table. He had given up practice in due course, only to be brought back out of retirement when war broke out. Many of the younger men had been called up to serve in the armed forces, and men like Dr Mallory had to fill in for them on the home front. The civilian population still needed medical care, especially those who lived in areas where there were bombing raids.

'I expect it will be a big funeral,' Maudie murmured.

'I imagine so. It will be at Midvale, of course, on Thursday. Harold and I intend to go; can we offer you a lift?'

'Yes, please. It might be a bit awkward getting there on time if I went by bus.'

★　★　★

Maudie did not possess a black coat to wear for the occasion. There was one good thing about it being a doctor's funeral, though; she could turn up in her uniform and not look out of place. She would give her gabardine overcoat a good brushing and would look perfectly decent. Very likely other nurses would do the same.

In recent years, prior to the implementation of the National Health Service, Dr Mallory had relied on the district nurses and midwives to fill in for him in the country areas. While his mind had been sharp enough, he was becoming physically frail and unable to travel around the countryside as much as he could have wished. Thus he depended on these nurses to assess the needs of their patients on his behalf. Depending on the circumstances, those in need might be told to report to his surgery at Midvale, or to attend the cottage hospital.

Maudie had enjoyed the extra duties that had come her way and her patients, for the most part, had been grateful for her ministrations. She had come to know them well in her trips around the district on her trusty bicycle, and felt herself thoroughly at home wherever she went.

That had changed after the National Health Act of 1948. Two younger doctors had bought out Dr Mallory's practice, leaving him free to bow out. Dr Donald Dean had taken over the old doctor's house and surgery at Midvale, and his partner, Dr Leonard Lennox, had settled in Llandyfan, opening a surgery in the converted gatehouse on his aunt's estate. And that, thought Maudie grimly, was a whole other story!

4

Maudie called in at the village shop in order to purchase a bluebag. Her bed linen was beginning to look a little dingy and the weather was so miserable that there was no chance of seeing a bit of sun strong enough to bleach them white again. In fact there was really no point in hanging anything out on the line at all. It was cold enough to freeze the sheets, and at the end of the day she had to bring them back in, stiff as boards, and hang them up in the scullery, where they thawed out and dripped mournfully onto the flagstone floor like a giant's tears.

Mrs Hatch, who was the Llandyfan postmistress as well as being the owner of the shop, greeted Maudie cheerfully. She knew everyone's business and seemed to think it her mission in life to keep everyone informed of whatever she could find out.

'What do you think about the new

doctor, then?' she asked. 'Good news, isn't it?'

'What new doctor?'

'You mean you haven't heard? I'd have thought you'd be the first to know. A Gloucestershire chap, I heard, coming to take over from Dr Lennox.'

Maudie stared at the postmistress in astonishment. 'You don't mean someone's coming to take over the gatehouse?'

'Why, yes.'

'I think you must have got hold of the wrong end of the stick, Mrs Hatch. The last I heard Mrs Beasley was selling up and moving away, and Dr Lennox was about to go abroad.'

Some months earlier Dr Lennox, who was Mrs Beasley's nephew, had been falsely accused of murder. Mrs Beasley and Maudie had actually been cornered by the real culprit, who happened to be another nephew, one Brian 'Bingo' Munroe. Salvation had come in the person of a distraught husband who was trying to locate Maudie for his wife, who was about to give birth. Munroe had run off, leaving the frightened women unhurt.

'Oh, that was the plan, all right, Nurse, but Cora Beasley hasn't had any luck selling her place. Nobody wants those great big houses anymore, you see. The only offer she had came from a builder chap who was going to tear the place down and build a lot of little rabbit hutches instead. You know the sort of thing: little jerry-built boxes all crowded in close together. Not the sort of thing we want in Llandyfan at all. That would attract all sorts of riff-raff, that would. And what would happen to those farms she rents out? You'd have a lot of yobbos racing all over the place on them motor scooters, putting the cows off their milk. So Cora said she'd just have to stay on and try to live down the disgrace, that's all.'

'Poor Mrs Beasley has nothing to be ashamed of,' Maudie said.

'Except that Bingo Munroe is her nephew, Nurse, and he did kill that poor girl that was in love with his cousin.'

'It's a shame that Dr Lennox has decided not to stay,' Maudie said. 'He's a very good young doctor, and everybody liked him. I thought highly of him myself.'

'Ah, but it didn't do him any good, getting accused of murder like that,' Mrs Hatch retorted. 'You know what people round here are like. No smoke without fire, that's what they'd say. No, he's better off starting up again somewhere new, preferably abroad.'

'In a leper colony or somewhere like that?' Maudie asked, but it was never any use being sarcastic with Mrs Hatch because she just didn't get it. 'I've come for a bluebag,' she said, hoping to change the subject.

'Sorry, I'm all sold out. They've been on order for weeks but I'm still waiting. The thing is, they're too old-fashioned now. I wouldn't be surprised if they went out of style altogether one of these days. I could sell you a bottle of bleach, now. That should get your things nice and white again.'

'No, thanks. I don't care for the smell.'

'Fancy that! I should have thought you'd be used to smells, you being a nurse.'

'There are smells and smells, Mrs

Hatch. What did you say that new doctor was called?'

'I didn't, but his name's Ransome. Dr Julian Ransome.'

Maudie's heart gave a painful lurch. No! Was it possible? Fate couldn't be that unkind, surely? Of course there were lots of people called Ransome, and there might be numerous doctors among them. But what were the odds of the newcomer being the man who had broken Maudie's heart so cruelly when she was a trainee nurse?

She clung to the notion that this particular Dr Ransome was a Gloucester-shire man. Her Julian Ransome had come from Surrey, and she knew she wasn't mistaken about that. When you are young and in the throes of first love, you absorb every possible fact about the object of your affections, and she had soaked up everything he had told her about himself. His parents and younger sister lived somewhere in Godalming, and in antici-pation of meeting them some day she had gone to the library and looked the place up in the atlas.

Veronica. That was his sister's name: younger than Julian and pony-mad. Maudie had even bought the girl a card for her fifteenth birthday and given it to Julian to post. It had a lovely big horse on it, looking over a fence. She wondered now if the girl had ever received it.

'Are you all right, Nurse?' Maudie suddenly became aware that Mrs Hatch was staring at her curiously.

'What? Oh, sorry! I was far away for a minute there.'

'Thinking about lover-boy, were you?'

'Yes, something like that.' She pulled herself together.

'I hear your fiancé is going away again,' Mrs Hatch said. 'You want to pin him down to a firm date for the wedding before he changes his mind.'

Now how on earth had the woman found out about that? Dick had only just come to a decision himself. Really, if they ever held another church fête — not at all likely after the disastrous one of two years ago — then Mrs Hatch would do very nicely as a replacement for the unfortunate fortune-teller who had been murdered in her tent.

'We do have a date,' Maudie said firmly. 'At least, we know it will be in June. I just have to see the vicar to firm up the actual day.'

'Let me know in plenty of time,' Mrs Hatch said. 'I shall buy a new hat for the occasion.'

Oh, dear! Maudie hadn't even considered the possible guest list. She was well known in the district, of course, and perhaps a lot of people would kindly want to wish her well for the future. Added to that, it was traditional for the local women to wait near the church door to see the bride and groom emerging after the service. But they couldn't invite everyone to the reception that followed. Weddings were expensive. How were they going to manage? Maudie's parents were no longer living and she would have to be responsible for all the arrangements herself. Could she ask the Women's Institute to cater for a buffet meal, with sandwiches and tray bakes? And what about the cake?

'My goodness, Nurse, you are in a dream today!'

'I've got a lot on my mind, Mrs Hatch. Attending Dr Mallory's funeral, for one thing. And if this new Dr Rowbottom is coming, I suppose I'll have to break him in, take him round the area and introduce him to his patients. It's all very time-consuming and I still have my mothers and babies to think of.'

'Ransome, Nurse. His name is Ransome. You must be thinking of Sid Rowbottom, the old boy at the cottages near Hill Farm. Used to be a road mender for the council, before your time. Why, I remember when his old dad . . . '

Maudie had suffered enough. She raced out of the shop, letting the door swing to behind her. Mrs Hatch watched her go. 'Well, I never! What's bitten her?' She stepped forward to greet a newcomer to the shop.

'Where's she off to?' the woman demanded. 'Somebody in labour, is there?'

'Don't ask me, Mrs Forbes! She's like a bee on a hot griddle today. I couldn't get

34

a sensible word out of her.'

'Ah, that'll be wedding jitters, I suppose. If she knew what I know about marriage, she wouldn't be in such a hurry to walk down the aisle! And I wouldn't marry a bobby, not for all the tea in China. It's a dangerous job, that is. Her poor hubby! He might get beaten up by thugs, or shot dead, even, and she'd be a widow before she'd hardly got started. She'd have a pension, though, I suppose, and that's something.'

'This is Llandyfan, Mrs Forbes, not Chicago.'

'And we've had three murders here in three years, haven't we?'

'True enough. Let's hope we don't see any more. Now, what can I do for you today?'

Mrs Forbes consulted her list. 'I need cream of tartar, scouring pads, and something nice to go with a cup of tea.'

'I've got some nice Marie biscuits, just in off the carrier's van. Or Rich Tea, if you prefer those.'

'I don't suppose you've any chocolate bikkies? I've got my grandson coming for his tea and I do like to treat the kiddie.'

5

The church was already full when Maudie and the Blunts arrived at St Mary's in Midvale, but fortunately she and Joan were escorted to reserved seating. Harold Blunt, as vicar of one of the churches in the area served by the late Dr Mallory, was taking part in the funeral service, and his wife was treated with the dignity due to his office. Maudie wasn't too sure about sitting in a front pew, but it was either that or stand up at the back of the church for the duration of what promised to be a lengthy ordeal.

Although she was a regular churchgoer, more or less, she hated to sit in front where everyone could see what she was up to. A funeral service wasn't like regular matins or evensong. What if she knelt, or stood up, or sat down at the wrong times? And worse, what if she made a mistake and those behind her followed her lead? Chaos might ensue. She comforted herself with the thought that Mrs Blunt would surely know what to do, and Maudie could follow her lead.

She supposed that one funeral was much like another. There would be hymns and scripture readings and the local vicar or his appointees would get up and say nice things about the deceased person. Well, that was all right in Maudie's book. Old Doc Mallory deserved anything good they would say about him. He had led a full and useful life, even coming back into the working world during the war when he should have been happily retired, growing roses or something.

She glanced across to the pews on the right side of the aisle, where the relatives of the deceased would normally be seated, sniffling, or bravely holding back tears. An elderly woman sat there, ramrod-stiff, with one gloved hand on the rack holding the hymnals as if to save herself from falling over. That, Maudie supposed, was probably the late doctor's sister. She seemed to be accompanied by another woman, possibly a friend or neighbour; as far as Maudie knew the sister was unmarried, which was why the doctor had elected to spend his retirement staying with her.

The procession was coming now, led by a small boy in a white surplice carrying a large brass cross. With his halo of untidy blond curls he looked like a little angel, although the effect was somewhat spoiled by the battered plimsolls she could see protruding from under his gown.

At long last the pallbearers shouldered the coffin and the congregation filed out to the churchyard, where the remains of the late doctor were reverently lowered into the ground. A stiff east wind caused Maudie to draw the collar of her Burberry up around her chin and she hoped that the church ladies would be providing plenty of strong, sweet tea when all this was over. Never mind ashes to ashes, dust to dust; the onlookers stood in danger of being turned into blocks of ice.

'You look like a nurse,' said a male voice as Maudie took her place at one of the long tables in the parish hall, gratefully curling her numb fingers around a steaming cup of tea.

'Not only that, I am a nurse,' she replied, smiling at the man who had appeared at her elbow. He was in his twenties, she thought: of medium height, with sandy hair and a slightly crooked nose.

He nodded. 'You worked for my father, did you?'

'Your father? No, I'm the midwife at Llandyfan.'

'Oh. Seeing you in the church, I thought you must be from Midvale.'

'You wouldn't be Dr Ransome, I suppose?' she murmured hopefully.

'No, who's he?'

'Oh, a new doctor who has just bought into what used to be Dr Mallory's practice here. In partnership with Dr Dean, who has the surgery here in Midvale now. Look, if you want to talk to someone who worked with Dr Mallory, that's his office nurse-cum-receptionist over there, in the navy blue suit with the pillbox hat.'

'Thanks! I'd better catch her before she

gets away.' He sped off, leaving Maudie to enjoy her tea. She wasn't alone for long, for Mrs Blunt soon arrived with the doctor's sister in tow.

'May I introduce Miss Mallory?' she said. 'This is Nurse Rouse from Llandyfan.'

Standing up, Maudie extended a hand. 'How do you do?'

'How do you do? Won't you join me? I see someone approaching with a plate of sandwiches. I'm sure you could do with something. This must be a difficult day for you.'

'It is indeed,' Miss Mallory sighed, sinking down onto the chair Maudie pulled out for her. 'People have been so kind, and have said such nice things about my poor brother, but I do find it exhausting talking to them all. And the thought of going back to my empty house after having him staying with me there is quite daunting.'

'Don't you have anyone who can come and stay with you? A cousin, perhaps, or a niece?'

'I'm afraid I'm all alone in the world

now. My brother and I are the only surviving members of our little family, and neither of us ever married. He was always too busy with his medical practice and I lived in India for many years. I was a missionary, you know.'

When Maudie excused herself to visit the cloakroom she noticed the sandy-haired young man leaning against the wall beneath a large reproduction of Holman Hunt's famous painting, 'The Light of the World'.

'Did you manage to catch up with Miss Holmes?' she asked, more for something to say in passing than because she was interested.

'Oh, yes, but she wasn't much help.'

'Oh, dear. That doesn't sound like Miss Holmes. I expect she's not quite herself today. Naturally she'll be quite upset over Dr Mallory's death.'

His reply quite took Maudie's breath away. 'Oh, we're all upset, Nurse. Me especially.'

'I'm sorry to hear that. Did you know him well?'

'Did I know him well? I should do! He was my father.'

Maudie longed to get to the bottom of this, but unfortunately three cups of tea had worked their magic and she was forced to barge into the lavatory without further ado. When she emerged the young man had disappeared.

* * *

'I do feel sorry for poor Miss Mallory,' Joan Blunt said when they were seated in the vicar's old Rover on their way back to Llandyfan. 'Still, I'm afraid there comes a time when we do find ourselves alone in the world, if our loved ones have gone before us. It does seem a shame that she should end her days in loneliness after contributing so much to others through her missionary work.'

'Something rather odd happened just before we left,' Maudie piped up from the back seat. Her friend twisted around to look back at her. 'I met a chap who claimed to be Doc Mallory's son.'

'Are you sure you understood him correctly, Nurse? As you know, Dr Mallory was never married. That was mentioned in his eulogy.'

'I expect that the man in question was a godson,' the vicar put in, swerving to avoid a small dog that had dashed into the road in front of his car. 'Did you see that? I do wish people would keep their dogs in check. That little brute could have had us in the ditch if I hadn't had my wits about me.'

'Yes, dear,' his wife told him. 'It was very clever of you to avoid it. Now, then, Nurse — do tell us more.'

'There's nothing more to tell. That's what's so maddening. I had to leave him for a minute or two, and when I came back he'd vanished.'

'Perhaps he's a professional funeral-goer,' the vicar murmured.

'What on earth is that?' Maudie wondered. 'Someone you pay to attend a funeral to make up for the lack of mourners?'

Mrs Blunt laughed. 'You mean like getting your friends to attend the performance of a new play to prevent there being too many empty seats? Hardly that. I think that what Harold means is someone like old Miss Craven. She attends every funeral that comes along, whether she knows the deceased person or not. I think she enjoys the company, poor old dear. She's a lonely soul.'

But Maudie couldn't see why a man of his age would want to do such a thing. If he was short of company surely he could take up a sport, or attend night classes or something. And why would he lie about being Dr Mallory's son? Something wasn't right, and it annoyed her to think that she might never know the truth of the matter.

6

Maudie carefully reached into the oven to check on the hotpot she was making. Just as she did so a thunderous rapping came at her front door, making her jump. Her right hand touched the shelf of the oven and she withdrew it quickly, cursing under her breath. She switched off the cooker and turned to the sink, where she let cold water stream over the affected part.

The pounding came again, this time accompanied by an angry male voice. 'All right, keep your hair on! I'm coming. I'm coming!'

She flung the door open to find Raymond Pugh on the step, his face contorted with fury. 'What took you so long? You must come at once, Nurse! It's Dilys. She's gone into labour!'

Maudie was used to distraught fathers and she forgave him for his unpleasant tone. 'Yes, of course I'll come at once, Mr

Pugh, but I shouldn't think there's anything to worry about. This may be false labour. It often happens, you know. It's just nature's way of preparing the muscles to give birth.'

'The child is coming, I tell you! My wife slipped and fell off a step ladder and it must have jarred something inside her.'

'What on earth was she doing up a ladder in her condition?' Maudie demanded to know. 'Oh, never mind. What's done is done. You go and wait in the car while I fetch my bag. I'll be with you in two shakes of a lamb's tail.'

It took her no time at all to wash her hands and gather up the things she needed, but when she emerged from the house the car was gone. 'Well blow me down! The miserable so-and-so has driven off and left me!' She was still muttering to herself as she dragged her bike out of the lean-to at the back of her cottage and set off into the drizzle. Maudie told herself that a charitable person would have put this down to the man's concern for his wife, in which he had overlooked the fact that the midwife had to be given a lift to his home, but in this case the chap was just being plain awkward. A difficult customer, and no mistake!

When she finally reached her patient's side Maudie saw at once that this was no false alarm. The second stage of labour had already started and Dilys was groaning in pain. In a very short time they would have an eight-months baby on their hands.

'I'll be off, then,' Pugh announced. 'Be so good as to pop into the Royal Oak when it's all over and let me know what we've got.'

Maudie drew herself up to her full height. 'I shall not be popping in anywhere, as you put it, Mr Pugh. I am not the angel Gabriel and I've left my horn at home. I want you to take yourself down to the phone box and call for an ambulance. Is that clear?'

'There is absolutely no need to waste money on an ambulance, Nurse! Child-birth is a perfectly natural condition, and once my wife stops howling like a banshee she'll be quite all right.'

Through gritted teeth Maudie explained that the baby had not come to term and would possibly need to spend time in an incubator. The Pughs' bedroom was frigid and the waiting treasure cot would not provide the protection the immature little lungs needed. 'And I shall have to decide whether your wife needs to go into hospital as well. And for your information, the cost of the ambulance is covered under the National Health Service.'

'I suppose it's all right, then.'

'Just go, Mr Pugh, will you!'

All went well with Mrs Pugh's delivery, and soon afterwards she happily cradled her newborn son while Maudie went to put the kettle on.

'He hasn't got much hair, has he, Nurse? I mean, he won't always be bald, will he?'

Maudie laughed. 'Give him six months and he'll have a thatch like a coconut. A couple of years ago I brought another little egghead into the world, and you should see him now. I had to laugh when we showed the child to his five-year-old big brother. Little Albie set up a howl and when we asked him what the matter was he sobbed that somebody had stolen all the baby's hair and teeth!'

After the ambulance attendants had settled the new baby into a portable incubator, Maudie looked down at Dilys Pugh and frowned. 'I don't like leaving you alone,' she said. 'Isn't there someone who can come in and stay for a bit? A neighbour, perhaps?'

'There isn't anybody I can ask. We haven't got to know people yet, you see. I'll be all right, Nurse, now that the baby is being looked after. All I want to do is sleep.'

'Your husband should be here, really. Perhaps I'd better look in at the Royal Oak and ask him to come home.'

'Please don't do that, Nurse. He'll come home eventually. He always does.'

'Well, if you're quite sure. I'll pop in tomorrow and see how you're getting along.'

By the time Maudie set out for home, the rain was coming down in torrents and she could hardly see where she was going. There seemed to be no point in trying to cycle through that lot so she trudged along with her head down, longing to get home and into a warm bath.

'I could wring that man's neck!' she thought fiercely. What with one thing and another she felt like giving him a piece of her mind, but she was in no mood to make a detour to the Royal Oak.

She was saddened to think of poor little Mrs Pugh alone in her house, separated from her new baby, even if it was all for the best if the child was to do well. While it was the usual thing for husbands to keep out of the way during labour and delivery, most were delighted to reappear when it was all over, to meet their new son or daughter and to at least give their wives a kiss and a hug. Why was Raymond Pugh such a cold fish? Somebody ought to sort him out, and Maudie was the woman to do it, but she had to be careful. It wasn't wise to come between husband and wife unless actual abuse was suspected. Interference could make a difficult situation worse.

Letting herself into her darkened cottage, Maudie felt a sudden longing to see Dick. He at least was warm and supportive, and it would be wonderful to have him to come home to once they were married. That was if she continued her job, of course.

She pulled off her soaking shoes, noting with annoyance that the dye had run and her stockings had black streaks on them. They had rubbed her feet and she had the beginnings of a blister on one heel.

Remembering her hotpot, she opened the now-cool oven, only to find that the food had gone dry. Possibly it could be saved, she thought. At least it hadn't burned, but she didn't fancy it now. Perhaps tomorrow it could be resuscitated with the help of a little Bisto gravy.

Meanwhile, she would have a long soak in a lavender-scented bath, and if she could summon up the energy after that she would make herself a plate of scrambled eggs and take it up to bed with her. No, on second thought, two boiled eggs would have to do. No horrid saucepan to clean later!

7

By morning Maudie had recovered her customary good humour. The sun was shining, and with any luck the day would warm up a little. She decided to call on the vicar's wife before starting out on her rounds.

Joan Blunt greeted her cheerfully. 'I hear the Pughs have had a little boy. That's nice for them.'

'News travels fast.'

'Oh, Harold was visiting old Mrs Carson when her grandson called in to see her. He works as an ambulance attendant, you know. She can't get out much and she likes to hear all the news. He told her they'd just transported the Pughs' little boy to the cottage hospital. I hope he'll be all right.'

'I expect so. He just put in an appearance a bit early, that's all.'

'And the mother? How is she?'

'I'm on my way to check on her now. I

think she's rather down in the dumps, poor soul. They haven't been here long and I suspect she's a bit lonely. Her husband works over at Midvale so she's alone all day, and I expect she's fretting over the baby. This is the time when mother and child should be bonding with each other, but it could be weeks before she gets to hold him in her arms again.'

'Would she like me to pop in, do you think?'

'I'm sure she'd appreciate that. And perhaps you could wave your magic wand and find her a friend or two. When the mother-and-baby group starts up again I'll encourage her to attend, but meanwhile she really does need some support.'

'Of course, and I'll tell you what I'll do. I'll mobilise the Mothers' Union and get them to take it in turns to deliver a casserole or something for the evening meal while little Mrs Pugh is recovering in bed. I'm sure she won't feel like getting up to do the cooking.'

'No, indeed. She should have her nine days' rest like everyone else. It's good of you to do this, Mrs Blunt. Are you sure the ladies won't mind the extra work?'

'They'll be cooking for their own families. It won't hurt them to whip up a bit extra while they're at it.'

Maudie felt a warm glow inside. People in country places were always so willing to rally round when someone needed help. 'Right then, I'll be off. And if you could pop in and get to know her, that would take a weight off my mind.'

'Speaking of introductions, Nurse, I've a message to pass on. Cora Beasley is planning a reception of sorts on Wednesday evening so that people can meet the new doctor, Julian Ransome. She hopes you can be there.'

'Oh.'

'What's the matter? Aren't you curious to meet him?'

'Um, I suppose so. Who else is invited?'

'It's a sort of open house, I think. Between you and me and the gatepost, I think she's concerned that she might be snubbed if she only asks certain people. After what happened last year she's feeling rather insecure, and if she throws the event open to everyone there should be enough people to cover any obvious gaps in the ranks.'

'Poor woman. I think she's being very brave.'

'Only on the outside, I'm afraid. She's being very stiff-upper-lip and all that, but underneath it all she's quite unhappy. She's even volunteered to step down as President of the Mothers' Union, but I refused to accept her resignation. It's not her fault that Bingo went off the rails. Harold heard that the chap has been found not guilty by reason of insanity. He isn't fit to stand trial.'

Maudie shuddered. Having narrowly escaped death at the hands of that same Bingo, she wondered what would become of him. With any luck he was probably locked up in a secure facility, but for how long? Would he be deemed cured after a few years behind bars, and released on the say-so of some misguided psychiatrist? In her experience, those who doctored the mind were sometimes as mixed up as the patients they served.

* * *

Maudie found Dilys Pugh in good spirits, still buoyed up with the euphoria that follows a successful childbirth. 'Have you had any breakfast?' Maudie asked her.

'Ray brought me a cup of tea before he left for work, but I wouldn't mind another one.'

'Right, then. Let's have a look at you, and then we'll get you washed. After that I'll make you some tea and toast, if you can manage that.'

'That would be lovely.'

As she worked, Maudie explained to her patient what was in store for her. 'The vicar's wife said she'll pop in to see you later on. Her name is Joan Blunt, and she's organising the Mothers' Union to deliver something for your tea over the next few days.'

Tears welled up in Mrs Pugh's eyes. 'That is so kind!'

'Well, your husband will be hungry when he comes in from work, and you're not up to going to the shops, are you?' Maudie told her briskly.

'No, I'm afraid not. I meant to get a few tins in, for quick meals when the time came: beans on toast, soup, that sort of thing. Only, the baby came early and I was caught out.'

'No harm done,' Maudie assured her. 'Why not make up a shopping list and give it to Mrs Blunt when she comes? She can drop it off with Mrs Hatch, and there's a boy who makes deliveries on a bicycle after school. Problem solved!'

Maudie's next call was to an elderly man whose married daughter had asked her to make a visit. He lived in a pretty little cottage on the outskirts of the village. Although she had often cycled past it she had never been inside and was eager to see what the interior was like.

It took her patient quite some time to shuffle to the door, but at last it was thrown open to reveal a white-haired man who regarded her with suspicion.

'Whatever it is you're selling I don't want none!' he informed her.

'Don't your recognise me, Mr Pratt? I'm Nurse Rouse. Your daughter asked me to call.' She realized she knew him by sight, having seen him hobbling his way to the Royal Oak from time to time.

'Eh?'

'Your daughter. Mrs Phee? She asked me to look in on you.'

'What?'

'Look, can we go inside? It's a bit nippy standing out here in this wind.'

Reluctantly he stepped aside, and she followed him into a tiny lobby cluttered with shabby coats and a muddy pair of wellingtons. Then they were inside a kitchen-cum-living room in which a smoking fire provided a certain amount of heat. The sink was filled with dirty crockery, and a grease-filled frying pan sat on the cooker, bearing mute witness to the fact that Mr Pratt had eaten a meal of sausages and eggs not long before. At least the old boy wasn't going hungry. Too many old folks neglected themselves and subsisted on a diet of tea and biscuits.

'I suppose you want a cup of tea!' he grumbled.

'No, I don't, Mr Pratt, thank you. I've just had one.'

'Well, I do. Put the kettle on, gal!'

Smiling, Maudie did as she was told. Filling the battered kettle, she asked him to describe what was causing him some concern. 'Your daughter tells me you're in pain most of the time.'

'It's just me rheumatics. Got to expect that at my age. Spent time in the trenches in the Great War, didn't I? Up to my knees in mud a lot of the time. That didn't do me no good at all.'

'No, I don't suppose it did.'

'Of course, it was me own fault. I had to go and join up when I needn't have gone at all. Forty-five I was, more fool me! Trouble was, I looked younger than me age, see, and some woman comes up to me in the street and pins a white feather on me. After that I had to fight for king and country, didn't I? No dratted woman calls Josh Pratt a coward and gets away with it.'

Maudie had to admire the spunky old man, and she decided to sit down with him and have a cup of tea after all. There might not be much she could do for his aches and pains other than prescribe something he could rub his joints with, but at least she could provide him with a bit of cheerful company.

'What about you, Nurse? Did you serve in the last lot? We had a lot of young girls looking after us out in Flanders. Don't know how we'd have managed, else.'

'No. I tried to join up, but they wouldn't have me.'

'What was wrong with you, then? Not properly qualified or summat?'

'Oh, I was qualified, all right, but I'm a midwife, you see. They said I was needed here, among the civilian population.'

'Ah. Not too many midwives needed over there, I suppose. But why did you want to go at all, Nurse, when you could have stayed safe at home, and no harm done? All those young gals joining up: ATS, WAAFs, Wrens, all them funny names. It ain't right nor natural. Them Land Gals, now; that's another matter.'

'That's a story for another day,' Maudie told him. 'And as for joining the women's services, that's all behind us now, and I don't see how we could have won the war without them.'

8

Maudie laboured up the long drive to Mrs Beasley's house, regretting that she'd decided not to come in uniform. The skirt of her woollen frock was riding up over her knees; her legs, in their sheer stockings, were turning blue with cold; and her high-heeled court shoes kept slipping off the pedals. The day was so windy that she had been forced to wear a headscarf, which meant that her hair would probably be flat when she arrived. Still, what was good enough for Princess Elizabeth was good enough for her! She had seen photos of that lovely young woman wearing such a scarf when out riding her horse.

Sheer vanity had driven Maudie to come dressed to kill. She needed the confidence that smart clothes would give her when she faced this Dr Ransome, if indeed he turned out to be her former boyfriend. Words of a hymn darted through her mind. 'Gird your armour on, stand firm everyone . . . ' Yes, she would need to face him coolly, showing that she no longer cared.

It seemed that half of Llandyfan and the surrounding district had turned out to meet the new doctor. The house was crowded with people of all ages, including several pre-school children who were getting their fingers slapped by irate mothers for fiddling with things that didn't concern them.

Maudie caught up with one little boy just as he was about to yank on a lace tablecloth that would have brought dozens of cups and saucers crashing to the floor.

'If you touch that again, my lad, Father Christmas won't come,' she whispered. He stared up at her with his lip wobbling.

'He's already been,' he said at last. 'So there!'

'Ah, but there's always next year,' she told him. 'Now run along and find Mummy. She's looking for you.'

'No, she isn't!'

'She will when you've got a smacked bottom and she hears you yelling,'

Maudie told him. His mouth dropped open and he turned and ran.

'That's right, Nurse; you show the little tinker what's what. There's a few here could do with a good hiding, and that's a fact!' She turned to find Len Frost, landlord of the Royal Oak, at her elbow. She laughed,

'Oh, he's just bored, I expect. This is not really the place for children, but I suppose his mother had nobody to leave him with.'

'Ah! Now where is that dratted doctor? I need to get back to the pub. I didn't want to come in the first place, but our Dora made me. Got to show willing, she says. Willing for what? I'll see him soon enough if I have to go to his surgery.'

Maudie suspected that most of the people here felt the same. They probably had other reasons for coming. Some were curious to see how Cora Beasley was bearing up. Others wanted to get a look inside the manor house, which under normal circumstances they would never be able to do. Some, no doubt, wanted to experience the scene of the crime, although the murder of the young woman a few months previously hadn't happened inside the house, but in a disused hut on the estate.

Somebody handed Maudie a cup of tea and she moved away from the table to make room for others. There was a blazing fire in the grate and she sidled closer to that, feeling the need for warmth.

From somewhere outside the sound of a high-powered car overpowered the muted chatter of the guests. 'It's him!' somebody called. 'He's here. The doctor's arrived.'

Moments later Maudie was staring across the room at Julian Ransome, trying to swallow the panic that fluttered in her stomach. Yes, it was him, all right! A few pounds heavier, perhaps, with the beginnings of a spare tyre around the middle, and the hair beside his ears showed a few silver streaks that gave him an air of distinction.

Well, she certainly wasn't about to gallop up to him, reminding the man of past associations! Mrs Beasley was shepherding him around the room now, introducing him to various people who were eager to shake his hand.

'Just like royalty,' Maudie noted. She knew that gracious expression of his, which he could put on when it suited him.

'And this is our midwife, Nurse Rouse,' Cora Beasley announced when it was Maudie's turn to be introduced.

The doctor inclined his head towards her. 'How do you do?' His gaze quickly turned towards Mrs Hatch, who was next in line. Maudie was left standing with her mouth open.

Well, what had she expected? A friendly smile, as he explained to Mrs Beasley that they'd met before? Or some acknowledgment of her existence, as in, 'How are you, Maudie? Long time no see?'

Had she just been snubbed? Surely he must have recognised her? It had been a few years but she couldn't have changed that much. And if nothing else, the name Maudie Rouse had to have rung a bell! They had gone out together for months and talked about marriage, for goodness' sake!

It had all started when Maudie was a third-year student nurse and Julian a houseman in the same hospital. A houseman was a qualified doctor who had to spend a further year at his training hospital before moving elsewhere. In the United States and Canada such doctors were called interns, which Maudie thought was a more sensible term, given the fact that female doctors were also known as housemen. Hospital discipline was such that relationships between student nurses and doctors were frowned upon. A third-year nurse might get away with dating a medical student, but woe betide the girl who caught the eye of a real doctor and dared to accept an invitation to go out with him. Maudie had tried to explain this to a former school friend, whom she'd met up with on one of her rare visits home.

'Cheek!' Mavis had cried, appalled at the very idea. 'Who do they think they are? You'd think these old hospitals would be glad to get anybody to do their dirty work, never mind interfering in people's private lives. What's wrong with a girl walking out with a young man, anyway? How do they expect you to find a husband if you can't even have a decent date?'

'I don't suppose they do want us to find husbands,' Maudie told her. 'After they spend three years training us they don't want us dropping out. Married women have to give up hospital work then, you see.'

'So what? They've had three years' work out of you for nothing, haven't they?'

No, Mavis would never be able to see eye to eye with hospital discipline and etiquette. Maudie still felt a flush of embarrassment when she remembered her first week in Women's Surgical after graduating from the Preliminary Training School. The telephone had rung just as Sister was escorting the surgeon, Mr Baines, on his ward rounds. (Surgeons were always known as 'Mister', even though they were highly qualified doctors.) Directed to answer the phone, and told that Mr Baines' presence was urgently required in theatre, Maudie had delivered the message to him, believing she'd done quite well. But the great man had barely disappeared through the doors of the ward before Sister turned on Maudie, her face contorted with fury.

'You will never, ever address any doctor or surgeon directly, is that clear? You speak to me, and I will relay the message to him! Is that clearly understood?'

'But Mr Baines was standing right beside you, Sister.'

'How dare you answer me back! If you cannot do as you are told, you will never make a nurse, Nurse!'

Sister hadn't bothered to lower her voice, and thirty-six pairs of eyes had focused on poor Maudie as the patients waited to see how she received this reprimand. Hot with shame, Maudie studied her clumsy black shoes while muttering, 'Yes, Sister. Sorry, Sister' — words she was doomed to repeat many times during the following three years.

Despite this unpromising start she had eventually reached the stage where she was allowed to speak to doctors in person, and that was when she had got to know Julian Ransome. On night duty she had been in charge of a thirty-bed women's medical ward, assisted by a junior. Coming in to check on one of his patients, Julian had stopped to chat up Maudie. This became a regular habit, with the two of them sitting in the darkened ward, talking in low voices and keeping a wary eye out for Night Sister, who might at any moment coming creeping in on her crêpe-soled shoes.

Maudie had graduated soon afterwards and she and Julian became an item, playing tennis together and going for long cycle rides in the surrounding countryside. Before long she found that she was falling deeply in love.

9

Maudie was making the most of her time with Dick, for he would soon be off to Hendon. He wasn't the best company because he always had his head in a book, trying to bone up on the requirements for his sergeant's exams. Still, at least he was with her, and she was glad to have his company on the occasional wintry evening he could spare to call on her, while she got on with her knitting.

Two nights after her reintroduction to Julian Ransome, Dick was at her cottage as usual when tragedy struck. Maudie was sitting beside the fire, half asleep, when the clock chimed ten. Yawning, she stretched and struggled to her feet, putting her knitting down on her little chair-side magazine rack. She knew that Dick would soon have to be on his way and he would need a fortifying hot drink before he set off in the cold on his motorcycle.

'Like a cup of tea before you go, Dick? Or I can do Ovaltine, if you prefer.'

Before he had a chance to respond they heard a car approaching, followed by a squeal of brakes and a thump.

'Something doesn't sound right,' Dick muttered, getting up and going to the door.

'Here, you can't go out in your shirt sleeves like that!' Maudie said, thrusting her arms into her winter coat. With Dick's overcoat over her arm and a powerful torch in the other hand, she followed him out. 'Can you see anything? Whoever it was is far away by now, I'm sure. Probably somebody who's had one too many in the Royal Oak, I expect.'

But Dick's attention was on a huddled form at the side of the road. 'Can you bring that light over here, Maudie? I think someone's been hurt.'

'It's the vicar,' she murmured, feeling for a pulse. 'There's some blood, but he's still alive. Dash back to the house and call 999.' But the resourceful Dick was already on his way.

The vicar moaned. Maudie bent closer. 'Can you hear me, Mr Blunt? It's me, Nurse Rouse. You've had an accident but you're going to be all right. We've sent for an ambulance and you'll soon be safely in hospital.'

'What's going on here? What happened?' Maudie looked up, recognising the Bensons, her neighbours, who had just arrived on the scene.

'It's the vicar. There's been an accident I'm afraid, but everything is under control.'

'We can't just leave him there!' Muriel Benson protested. 'Here, let's move him to the side.'

'No, Mrs Benson. I don't know the state of his injuries and moving him might do more harm than good.'

'But what if something comes round the corner? He'd get run over!'

'Of course, we can't let that happen. You take my torch, Mr Benson, and go down the street a bit, ready to flag down anyone who comes along. And have you any torches at home, Mrs Benson? We could do with some extra light here.'

The Bensons went to do as Maudie had asked, and she bent over the vicar again, praying that the ambulance would not be delayed.

'How is he?' Dick had returned at last.

'Still alive. I've got Seb Benson stationed down the street, ready to flag down anything that comes along. Is the ambulance coming?'

'It's on its way, and the Cottage Hospital has been alerted.'

'Good.'

'I'm going to pop over to the vicarage to fetch Mrs Blunt. She'll want to go with him in the ambulance. If they arrive before I get back, tell them to wait for her. That's if it's advisable to wait, of course.'

★   ★   ★

Mrs Blunt arrived, panting, just as they were loading her husband into the ambulance. 'Is he . . . I mean, he's not dead, is he?'

'He seems to be holding his own,' Maudie told her.

'Thank goodness! Oh, my poor Harold! I'm sorry I took so long. I was just getting ready for bed when Mr Bryant came, and I had to stop and get dressed all over again. I couldn't go to the hospital in my nightie, could I, although they're used to seeing nighties here, aren't they? Unless it's men, of course. They wear pyjamas.' She put a hand to her forehead, brushing back a stray lock of hair. 'Sorry, Nurse, I'm babbling.'

Maudie took her friend's arm gently. 'Come along, time to go.'

'Yes, yes, I see. Er, if I don't get back — I mean, if we have to stay at the hospital for a few days — will you look after Perkin for me? He's been fed this evening, of course, but he won't know what's happened to me, poor cat.'

Maudie assured her that the animal would be well cared for. 'You've locked up the house?'

'Yes, the key is under the flowerpot, as usual.'

Dick tut-tutted when he heard that, but he said nothing. The poor woman had enough to worry about without getting a reprimand for careless home security practices. However, when the ambulance had gone, taking the Blunts with it, he mentioned it to Maudie.

'It's asking for trouble, you know, leaving their key out where anyone could find it.'

'I can't see that it makes much difference. Most people don't bother locking their doors anyway, or at least they used not to. The murders we've had in the past few years have made some folks a bit jittery.'

'Exactly! I sincerely hope that you keep your doors locked at all times, Maudie.'

'Well, yes, I do,' she said, 'but only because I'm a nurse. I have pills and things that shouldn't fall into the wrong hands.'

But was she truly as careful as she might be? she wondered with a tinge of guilt. Her front door might well be locked, but when she was at home the back door seldom was. After all, she might have to dash out to the clothes line if it started to rain, or to bring in a scuttle full of coal in the evening. You couldn't live like a prisoner in your own home, could you?

'I hope Mr Blunt will be all right,' Dick said. 'Do you think he's badly injured?'

'No bones broken as far as I could tell, and there wasn't a lot of blood. He's probably concussed, though, and as for internal injuries, we shall have to wait and see. I'm guessing, though, that the car or whatever it was just hit him a glancing blow, and he wasn't actually run over.'

'We'll know more when the forensics team have had a look around,' Dick said. 'They should be here soon. Meanwhile you go on home, old girl. I'll wait here to show them what's what.'

'I hope you catch whoever did this!' Maudie said, her eyes flashing. 'Anybody can have an accident, but to hit someone and keep going without stopping to help is just plain evil.'

★   ★   ★

There were no confinements pending, so the next day Maudie caught the bus to the Cottage Hospital, anxious for news of the vicar, and to comfort her friend. At the same time she could drop in on the maternity unit and see how the Pugh baby was doing. His parents would be glad of a progress report, she was sure.

She found Joan Blunt at her husband's bedside. The vicar was trussed up with tubes everywhere. Maudie, of course, knew what each one was for, but the sight must be worrying for a layperson. Certainly, Joan Blunt looked tired and wan.

'How is he?' Maudie whispered.

'Oh, he's come round once or twice, and he seems to know me.'

'That's a good sign.'

'Is it? Last night they were talking about moving him to a larger hospital in case there was bleeding on the brain or something. Oh, Nurse! They may have to drill holes in his skull!'

'It may not come to that, Mrs Blunt. Let's just wait and see, shall we?' Inwardly Maudie cursed the unfeeling doctor who had frightened her friend before knowing if anything was certain. 'I'm so sorry that Mr Blunt has had this accident, but we must just hope for the best.'

Maudie was sure that Mrs Blunt would say something about praying for a happy outcome; she was a clergyman's wife, after all. But what the poor woman actually said startled her.

'An accident, was it? I'm not so sure about that! If you ask me, someone deliberately tried to run Harold down, and it's only by the grace of God that he wasn't killed outright!'

'Oh, surely not, Mrs Blunt.'

Joan Blunt nodded. 'We've been getting anonymous letters — at least, Harold has — telling him he's a murderer and he'll pay for his crimes.'

'Good gracious! Don't tell me there's a poison-pen writer in the village.'

'Not in the village, no. These were postmarked London. And they are addressed to Harold by name, Reverend H. Blunt, so this is not a random thing. The latest one says, 'Be prepared, the end is near.''

'Have you told the police?'

'No. Harold said it must be some poor

soul who isn't right in the head — someone who perhaps had his brain turned during the war or something — and we should just ignore it.'

'How do you know the writer is a man?'

'We don't, of course. But not many women own cars, do they?'

'The police must be told at once, Mrs Blunt. You really should have said something last night, you know. They need all the help they can get and it's not right to keep them in the dark.'

'I'd like to wait until Harold comes round, and see what he says about it.'

'And meanwhile this looney goes free, and comes back later to have another go? I don't want us to fall out over this but I'm sorry, if you are not going to tell the police, then I shall.'

'Oh, I suppose you're right, Nurse. I'm afraid I just can't think straight with poor Harold lying here.'

10

As soon as Maudie reached home she telephoned Dick.

'This puts a different complexion on it,' he told her. 'Did Mr Blunt give you the letters to show us?'

'I'm afraid not. I'm told that Mr Blunt chucked them on the fire.'

'Did Mrs Blunt give you any details?'

'Just that they were written in blue ink on ordinary cheap notepaper, the kind you can buy in any small shop. They weren't words cut out of newspapers or anything like that. As I said, they were postmarked London, only the Blunts couldn't think of anyone they might know there.'

'I hope you told her to keep any further letters they might receive, and hand them over to us at once.'

'A fat lot of good that'll do, now that poor Mr Blunt has already been mown down!'

'If he recovers from this attack the perpetrator may not leave it at that. He may come back for another go, and the vicar may not be so lucky a second time.'

'But who can it be?

'Some nutter. Sorry, Maudie, I must dash. See you soon.' Dick rang off, leaving Maudie feeling frustrated. She replaced the earpiece on its hook and stood motionless for a while, waiting for inspiration. None came.

Remembering her promise to feed the Blunts' cat, she hastened over to the vicarage, retrieved the key from under the flowerpot, and let herself into the house. Perkin came to greet her, complaining loudly.

She found a piece of cooked cod beneath an upturned dish in the larder. 'I hope this was meant for you, and not for your master's supper,' she told the cat, who by this time was wrapping itself around her legs, purring loudly. 'Still, if it was for him, he won't be needing it now, so you may as well have it.'

After chopping up the fish she put the dish down on the floor and the cat fell on it greedily. 'While I'm here I might as well have a look around,' she told Perkin, who made no demur. She had no idea what she was expecting to find — after all, she couldn't go poking around in private papers — but she could at least make sure that nobody had broken in during the Blunts' absence, and possibly was still lurking around.

Cautiously she made her tour of the house. The kitchen was tidy and cold, the stove having gone out overnight. Two washed mugs sat on the draining board; the Blunts had evidently enjoyed a milky drink before turning in for the night. At least, she knew that Joan Blunt had been getting ready for bed before the incident. But what had taken the vicar out onto the street at that time of night? Had he been lured out by a bogus phone call? His wife hadn't mentioned anything about that.

Upstairs, the double bed had already been turned down for the night, and a blue winceyette nightgown had been tossed on top of the eiderdown where its owner had left it after getting dressed again in haste.

Everything seemed to be as it should be, so she returned to the kitchen, where Perkin stared at her balefully. She knew what that look meant: 'Do you call this breakfast? How am I supposed to survive the day on that mingy little plateful?'

Smiling, Maudie regarded his portly frame. 'What am I going to do with you, Perkin? I can't keep running over here every half hour to feed you, and your mistress may not be back for a few days.' Perkin had been an indoor cat ever since an encounter with a fierce dog a few months earlier had sent him to the vet with painful injuries.

Well, there was nothing for it but to take the cat home with her. Where was his travel case likely to be? As she had guessed, it was in the cupboard under the stairs. She brought it out, blowing a layer of dust off the top.

'Come on, puss. Nice puss!'

Perkin glared at her. Maudie edged closer. The cat backed away. Maudie spoke in soothing tones as to a recalcitrant patient who declined to have an enema. Perkin spat.

She leaned over and picked the cat up in both hands. With surprising agility for such a sturdy animal, he twisted in her grasp. Having somersaulted to the floor, he shot underneath the sofa, hissing horribly. From there he peered out at her suspiciously.

'All right then, you little beast, stay here all on your own!' Maudie mumbled, sucking her thumb where the cat had scratched her. 'You can jolly well make do with hard tack for the rest of the day, because I shan't come running after you!'

Still muttering, she filled his dish from the bag of dry cat food she found in the kitchen cupboard, topped up his water bowl, and left.

★　★　★

On her way home she encountered the new postman, who greeted her cheerfully.

'Morning, Nurse!'

'Good morning, Bert!'

'How's the vicar, then? I heard somebody tried to do him in. Is that right?'

'He's doing as well as can be expected,' Maudie replied, giving nothing away, 'but as far as I know it was a hit-and-run accident. I don't suppose we'll know the whole story until the driver comes forward.'

'If he comes forward. Doesn't seem likely, though, does it? If the blackguard wouldn't stop to see what he'd done, why, his conscience won't prick him now. He'll be miles away and the police will never catch up with him.'

'Don't be too sure about that! Meanwhile I'll be seeing the Blunts tomorrow and I'll pass on your regards, if you like. Is there any post for them? I may as well take it with me.'

'Now you know I can't hand it over to a third party, Nurse. It has to go straight to the person it's intended for. Post office regulations.'

'Post office regulations my foot! Who treated your piles when you were in misery, Bert Harvey? Hand it over, there's a good chap.'

'Well, I suppose this is a special circumstance,' he began. 'It's probably all circulars anyway.'

Maudie held out her hand and he placed several envelopes and a copy of the *Church Times* on her palm.

'Bye, Nurse! TTFN!'

'TTFN!' she replied, using the old wartime acronym that stood for 'ta-ta for now'. Back then some people had been superstitious, believing that if you used the word goodbye it might bring bad luck. That goodbye might be final. A soldier could be killed on active service; a bomb falling on the house might wipe out a civilian.

She glanced over the post in her hand. A brown envelope bore the ominous words, 'On His Majesty's Service'. That looked like some sort of tax demand. Mrs Lewis, who as Maudie knew was visiting her sister in Wales, had probably sent the picture postcard with a view of Cardiff Castle. And then there was a cheap white envelope addressed to the vicar in wobbly blue letters. Maudie's heart leapt.

She peered at the postmark. It was rather smudged, but she was sure that what she could see indicated that it had come from London. Convinced that it must be another of the threatening letters Mrs Blunt had told her about, she wondered what it was best to do next. Much as she longed to know if she was right, she couldn't open it, of course. Nor could she go to the hospital twice in one day to hand it to Mrs Blunt. And there was always the possibility that the good lady would destroy the evidence, as her husband had done previously.

But time was of the essence in trying to trace the person who had made the attempt on the vicar's life. Maudie knew that she had to risk her friend's displeasure and notify the police at once. She broke into a trot, heading for home.

11

When Dick arrived to see Maudie that evening she pounced on him at once. 'What was in the letter? Was it from whoever has been threatening the vicar? Will it help you to trace the driver of the car?'

'Whoa — back, old girl! What's all this about a letter?'

'It came for the vicar this morning. I telephoned you at once but they said you were out, so I gave a message to the dispatcher and a young constable called round to collect it.'

'First I've heard of it. And how did you get hold of it, anyway?'

'Mrs Blunt asked me to look in and feed the cat,' Maudie told him, glossing over the part where she had wrested the post from Bert Harvey. 'The postman called while I was there. I'll probably take the rest of it to the hospital the next time I go so I brought it home with me. I couldn't help noticing that envelope with a London postmark, so I thought I'd better hand it over to you people right away.'

'Very public-spirited of you, I'm sure!' Dick spoke sharply, but his eyes twinkled. He knew his Maudie all too well.

'Have they made any progress in finding out who ran down the vicar?' Maudie wanted to know. 'Oh, don't look so po-faced, Dick Bryant! I was here when we found him lying in his own blood, remember? I deserve to know what's going on, and you know I'll keep mum about it. Nursing ethics, and all that.'

'There's nothing much to say at the moment. All the garages in the area are being checked out in case the driver takes his car in for repairs. We found broken glass at the scene, which means that at least one headlamp was probably broken. But if I were that driver I'd probably lie low for a bit, or else take the car to a garage some distance away.'

Maudie groaned. 'Don't you think there should be a police guard at the hospital? What if the killer decides to strike again? Anybody could walk into that place, you know. All he has to do is wait until Mrs Blunt pops into the lavatory, then he picks up a pillow and smothers her husband, who is lying there unconscious. Easy as pie!'

'You've been reading too many Agatha Christies, old girl.'

'It's Dorothy L. Sayers now.'

'Yes, well, I'm not Lord Peter Wimsey, and neither are you. I think we'll leave the detecting to the experts, shall we? Now then, how was work today?'

Maudie pouted. 'Routine, really. I went to the hospital in the morning, of course, and then I made a few home visits; nothing special. Why do you ask?'

'No reason. I just wondered how you are getting along with that new doctor — Ransome, isn't it?'

'He hasn't actually started yet.'

'No? Well, I hope it all works out for you this time around. First you had that Dr Dean, who treated you like something the cat dragged in.'

'And then it was Dr Lennox, who was a

lovely man, but he was falsely accused of murder, and he's left the district,' Maudie added.

'So now, third time lucky. Let's hope this Dr Ransome will be everything a nurse could wish for,' Dick said. Grinning, he corrected himself hastily. 'Well, not quite everything! I don't want you falling for the chap!'

Maudie took a deep breath. 'Actually, Dick, there's something I should tell you. You see, I already know Dr Ransome. We both trained at the same hospital. We went out together when he was a houseman and I was a newly appointed staff nurse. It was years ago, of course. Before the war.'

'So what? I knew you must have had men friends before you met me. That's only to be expected . . . ' He paused and Maudie winced, waiting for him to say 'at your age', but when he spoke again he took her hand and gazed lovingly into her eyes. 'A woman as beautiful as you is bound to have had men lining up to take her out.'

'Fool!' she said, laughing.

'I've been out with other girls, of course, but until I met you I'd never found one I wanted to spend the rest of my life with.'

'I'm afraid it was a bit more than that with me and Julian,' Maudie said. 'I was head-over-heels in love with him at the time, and I thought he felt the same about me. He said he loved me, and we even discussed marriage, but then it all fell through.'

Even now she felt a pang, remembering the day that her hospital roommate had come in carrying a glossy magazine, the sort that printed photographs of society girls about to be married.

Wordlessly she pointed to the caption underneath the picture of the lovely blonde heiress draped in pearls, and Maudie had learned with an agonising shock that the prospective bridegroom was Dr Julian Ransome.

'Oh, well, water under the bridge, eh?' Dick murmured. 'I take it that it's all over now?'

'Oh, of course. Just one of those things, you know?'

'That's all right, then. But I hope it won't be too awkward for the pair of you having to work together now.'

'Oh, I shouldn't think so. He doesn't even remember me. At least, he didn't mention anything when we were introduced by Cora Beasley at the reception.' And that had stung.

When Dick had settled down to tackle his football pools and Maudie was ensconced in the fireside chair with her knitting, her thoughts flashed back to those heady days when she was young and desperately in love. Perhaps the writing had been on the wall back then — or had she been too besotted to read the signals? Julian had become quite angry with her when she'd refused to go with him on a weekend trip to Brighton, during which they'd be staying in a guesthouse, registered as Mr and Mrs Smith.

'Are you frigid or something?' he'd demanded, when she'd gently refused him. 'We love each other, don't we? We're going to be married, aren't we? So where's the harm in going away together?'

But Maudie had been brought up to believe that this was not the way for a decent girl to behave; and besides, if they were discovered she would face instant dismissal from the hospital and that would mean the end of her nursing career.

He had gone away in a fit of temper and she had been heartbroken when she later discovered that he had gone to Brighton anyway, taking with him another girl who didn't share Maudie's scruples. A nurse in her set, visiting her parents at their home in Brighton, had seen the pair together and had gleefully reported the sighting to Maudie.

'Coming out of the Lilacs Guesthouse they were, Rouse. My cousin's the receptionist there and she told me they were a honeymoon couple, a Mr and Mrs Smith. But I knew better, of course. Gillian said they were quite blatant about it all. They even ordered a bottle of wine to be sent up to their room, and they didn't put their noses outside the door all weekend. Don't look at me like that, Rouse! I thought you should know, that's all.'

Devastated, Maudie had tackled him about it. He had denied it at first, but faced with Nurse Bacon's evidence he was at last forced to admit what he had done.

'But I don't know what you are getting all het up about,' he blustered. 'I'm a free agent. You and I aren't married or anything. We're not even engaged, are we? Well, are we?' he demanded, when Maudie failed to reply to what she thought was a rhetorical question.

With the benefit of hindsight she knew now that she should have washed her hands of him then, but she was so much in love that she agreed to give him another chance. Somehow they'd picked up the pieces and their relationship limped on, but it had never been the same. Devastated though she was when she'd seen the announcement of his engagement, she knew somewhere deep inside that it was probably all for the best. Julian Ransome was one of those amoral men who could never be trusted. He had probably chosen his fiancée for the wealth she would bring to the marriage, and before long he'd be cheating on her as well.

This sad realisation did nothing to heal Maude's broken heart, so when she left the hospital to do her midwifery training she was glad of the long hours of work and study that went with that. She had just completed the course when war broke out, and she made up her mind to enlist in one of the women's services. Everyone had to register in any case, and once she was called up she wouldn't have any choice in the matter. She might as well sign on now. She was aware that she might be sent somewhere dangerous, but she didn't care. Life wasn't worth living without Julian.

12

The next day being Maudie's day off, she decided to take the bus to Midvale. She needed one or two things that the village shop could not supply, and she always enjoyed browsing in the bigger stores in the town. The skies were clear, with no threat of rain to come, so she bundled up well against the cold and set off.

The bus stopped across the street from what was now Dr Dean's surgery, and before she could think better of it Maudie dashed across and nipped into the waiting room. Miss Holmes looked up in surprise.

'Oh, is that you, Nurse? If you're looking for Dr Dean I'm afraid he's out on his rounds. A lot of our patients are down with coughs and colds and he doesn't want them coming in here, spreading their germs about.'

'Very right and proper. Actually, it isn't Dr Dean I've come to see. No, I thought

I'd call on Miss Mallory, just to make sure she's all right.'

Miss Holmes raised an eyebrow. 'Miss Mallory? Do you mean the doctor's sister?'

'That's right.' Maudie resisted the urge to say, 'No, you fool, the cat's mother,' but there was no point in alienating the receptionist. As it was, Miss Holmes seemed to be on the point of taking umbrage.

'She's a bit outside your district, isn't she? Nurse McGrath can manage very well if Miss Mallory needs to see anyone, and I very much doubt that she does. She has a neighbour who does a bit of shopping for her and, of course, Dr Dean will make her his top priority if she happens to fall ill.'

'Naturally,' Maudie said. While doctors and nurses always tried to do their best for each of their patients, they went the extra mile when it came to one of their own, and old Dr Mallory had served the community well for many years. By extension, his sister came in for the respect due to him for that.

'I'm afraid I didn't manage to have a word with Miss Mallory at the funeral,' she went on, crossing her fingers behind her back. 'And I really must express my condolences to the lady. After all, I've worked with her brother for many years now. Even before you came,' she added cattily. 'If you can give me directions to the lady's house I'll be on my way and let you get on.'

'Oh, very well. But it's a good two miles and you'll have to walk. The bus doesn't go out that way.'

* * *

The directions were simple enough, and after walking briskly for half an hour Maudie found herself at a pretty thatched cottage. When she opened the gate she saw that the garden had been put neatly to bed for the winter, but by the clumps of decaying foliage she could tell that the borders must present a riot of colour in the summer months. Close to the door a few snowdrops bloomed bravely and the sight cheered her.

There was no bell on the dark blue door, but there was a brass doorknocker shaped like a gargoyle's face. She lifted it and rapped three times. The door was flung open at once and the doctor's sister faced Maudie, annoyance all over her lined face.

'How many more times do I have to tell you? If you've come with the logs you've to go to the back door!'

'Er, I haven't brought logs,' Maudie explained. 'I'm Nurse Rouse, from Llandyfan.'

The older woman peered at her myopically. 'Well, of course you are! I'm so sorry. I've had my glasses off while putting cold cream on my face, and I don't see clearly without them. Do come in. I hope you won't mind being in the kitchen; only, I've just put a Victoria sponge in the oven and I don't want to forget it's there.'

Before settling herself on the proffered wooden chair Maudie glanced out of the window at the back garden, in which there was a lawn complete with a sundial and, further back, what appeared to be a vegetable garden, bare now except for some winter cabbages.

'I say, is that your log man now?' she murmured, having spotted a familiar figure moving a wheelbarrow about. Miss Mallory, her glasses restored to her face, came up beside her and peered out.

'Oh, no. That's Wilfred. He's been doing a few odd jobs for me.'

This gave Maudie the opening she'd been hoping for. 'Wilfred? That's your nephew, is it?'

'Nephew? Oh, no, Nurse. There was only my brother and myself in our little family, you know, and of course he was never married. Too busy with his medical practice, I'm afraid. If only he'd taken a partner early on it might have been different, but he was the sort of man who preferred to be a one-man band. It grieved him very much to sell up to those young doctors, Dean and Lennox, and when all that trouble arose with Dr Lennox he regretted it even more.'

'Poor Dr Lennox. None of it was his fault.'

'Perhaps not, but it certainly reflected

101

badly on the practice. It's my belief that it brought about my brother's untimely death.'

'I'm sorry to hear that, and that is why I'm here — to offer my condolences and to ask if there I anything I can do to help.'

'Thank you, Nurse; and no, I have everything I need at the moment. Besides, young Wilfred is here to run errands for me.'

'Is he a local boy?'

'No. I believe he said he comes from Devon.'

'And how did you come to find him? Did you apply for help at the labour exchange? Or did you place a card in the newsagents' window?'

Miss Mallory frowned. Maudie could tell that she was becoming annoyed. 'Really, Nurse, I'm not sure that this is any of your business! If you must know, he knocked on my door, asking if I wanted any gardening work doing. I thought he must be with the Scouts or something.'

'He's a bit old for Bob-a-Job. I don't mean to pry, but one has to be careful nowadays. I mean, one hears such awful stories about men who prey on elderly people, offering to do work as a means of gaining access to a house where there might be objects worth stealing.'

'I can assure you, Nurse, that I'm most careful when it comes to my own security. Of course I let him inside for a cup of tea, or to receive his wages, but I never leave him alone in the room for a moment. I don't even leave my handbag lying about. I count out the exact money owed to him and leave it on that shelf there. If he did help himself to that without my knowledge I should be annoyed, but of course it would not be stealing if he'd already accomplished the work and was merely collecting his wages.'

'I see,' Maudie said. Should she tell Miss Mallory why she was concerned about this Wilfred — if that was indeed his real name? The elderly woman was very proud of her late brother and she might become very cross indeed if she believed that his good name was being besmirched. If she chastised Maudie that wouldn't matter; but what if she lost her temper with the boy, demanding to know what he meant by claiming that he was Dr Mallory's son?

In her imagination Maudie could see the boy standing in front of his aged employer, holding some garden tool in his hand. Harsh words would be said and the boy told to leave at once. Frustrated at having been shown the door, the boy would raise his arm and bring the blunt instrument down on Miss Mallory's head. She would lie there in a pool of blood, possibly for days, until the postman or the milkman found her. Maudie shuddered.

'Are you all right, Nurse? You've gone quite pale. I'll get you a cup of tea as soon as I take my cake out of the oven, shall I?'

'Thank you, Miss Mallory. I'm afraid I do feel a bit weak.' She studied her hands, wanting to avoid the older lady's eye. No, it was better to say nothing. But for all she knew, the boy had already told the woman about his claim and his story had been accepted. There was no reason for Miss Mallory to share the tale with an outsider, and indeed, she might regard it as something to be kept secret from the world at large.

For the moment, then, Maudie would keep her own counsel — but she wouldn't leave it at that. There must be ways in which his story could be looked into.

13

Looking out of her bedroom window the next morning, Maudie noticed that an ambulance was drawn up in front of the vicarage. As there could be nobody there who might need help, it must mean that the vicar had been discharged from hospital. Cramming her uniform cap on her head and taking a last glance in the mirror of her dressing table, she hastily revised her plans for the morning. Updating her case notes could wait for another day.

Carefully pulling her front door closed behind her, she shook the doorknob just to make sure that the Yale lock had done its work. She had no wish to return home later to find someone lurking behind the door with murderous intent.

'Oh, there you are, Nurse!' Mrs Blunt seemed delighted to see her. 'We've turned up again, you see, like a couple of bad pennies.'

'Where is Mr Blunt? Would he like some help getting into bed?'

'He's had to dash to the lavatory. They've given him some sort of pills that cause him to go more often, if you know what I mean.'

'A type of diuretic, I expect. Has he fully recovered then?'

'On the face of it, yes, but he seems to have moments when he can't remember things. We've been told that the problem will probably right itself in time.'

'I expect so. Well, I shan't keep you now when you've just got back, but I'll pop in later just to make sure everything is all right.'

Mrs Blunt smiled. 'Yes, please do. And before I forget, I must thank you for looking after my poor Perkin. He must have wondered where we'd got to.'

'I was afraid he might get lonely, and I did try to take him to my place for the duration, but as soon as he saw the cat basket he went mad. He shot under the sofa and I wouldn't be surprised if he's still there. I'm not sure why that happened; he's known me long enough.'

107

'Ah, it was the cat basket that did it, Nurse. The last time he used it was when we took him to the vet to have him neutered. He must have been expecting more of the same!'

* * *

Maudie called in at her office in the parish hall to stock up on the few supplies she might need while on her rounds. She was about to lock and leave when the phone rang.

'Hello? Nurse Rouse speaking.'

'Is that the midwife?'

'Yes, this is Nurse Rouse.'

'Can you come at once? It's my Millie. She's in labour and I think she's rather poorly.'

Maudie frowned. She didn't know any Millie; there certainly wasn't one on her list of expectant mothers. The line crackled.

'Could you give me the address, please?' There was more crackling on the line. She would need to get on to Faults in the near future. 'Can you repeat that, please? Did you say Buttercup Lane? I don't think I . . . '

'The prefabs, Nurse! Please come quickly! I don't want her to die!' The line went dead. Either the woman had hung up in her agitation or they had been cut off.

Maudie ran for her bicycle, eager to get going. The prefabs were rows of temporary housing put up all over Britain to accommodate people who had been rendered homeless in the Blitz. Those built locally were on the other side of Llandyfan, on what had once been a working farm before its owner had passed on. His son was a clerical worker who hadn't wanted to continue farming, so the local council had acquired the land.

She cycled uphill through a stiff wind, her legs pumping painfully. If she didn't watch out she'd get a cramp in her calves, and then she'd have to dismount and limp along while pushing her machine. Why, oh why hadn't these people given her some advance warning of an impending confinement? And had the patient received any antenatal care? If she had, she certainly hadn't received it from Maudie.

Who was the woman who had called her? She had referred to the patient as 'my Millie', so probably she was the grandmother. No mention of the husband; maybe this was an unmarried mother. Oh well, that didn't matter to Maudie. She wasn't there to judge. Her job was to bring mother and baby safely through their ordeal, and that was that.

She reached Buttercup Lane at last and looked about her. She thought the woman had directed her to number forty-three, but the line had been so bad that she couldn't be sure. Fortunately a woman now appeared on the doorstep of that house and was signaling wildly to Maudie.

'Hello, Nurse! Thank you for coming so promptly. I'm just sorry you've had a wasted journey. It's all over, and Millie is just fine!'

'Oh, dear,' Maudie said, taken aback. 'I'd better come in, though, and take a look, just to make sure that all is well with mother and baby. And there will be some tidying up to do, I expect.' She had to make sure that the afterbirth had been safely delivered and carefully inspected, otherwise the mother could be in danger of a haemorrhage.

'Well, of course you're welcome to take a look, dear. Millie is so proud of her babies!'

'Babies? You mean there's more than one?' Maudie was appalled to think that the mother had just given birth to twins with this rather scatty woman as her only helper.

'Oh, yes, dear. Three! Such a clever girl, and this is only her first litter!'

'Litter?' Maudie began to see daylight. Not knowing whether to laugh or to cry, she followed the woman into a snug little room where a small black cat lay on a tartan rug in front of the fire, contentedly nursing three newborn kittens.

Maudie took a deep breath. 'You know, Mrs, er . . . '

'Barker, dear. Muriel Barker.'

'Well, Mrs Barker, I am not a veterinary nurse.'

The woman raised her eyebrows. 'I

never said you were, dear.'

'Yes, well, I'm a midwife, you see.'

'Yes, of course you are. That's why I called you. Poor Millie seemed to be having trouble, heaving and panting and mewing so piteously. I simply had to get help for her.'

'Then don't you think you should have called a vet?'

'I wanted to, but the phone box has been vandalised again and they've torn up the directory. So I got on to the exchange and she connected me with you.'

Maudie decided not to mention that the operator could just as easily have connected the woman with the vet's surgery, but possibly the woman had been misled by this talk of somebody in labour, just as Maudie had.

Mrs Barker seemed to be waiting for her to say something. What did she expect? Was Maudie supposed to congratulate her on the increase in her household? Or should she read the riot act? Offer forgiveness for the error?

'You know,' Maudie said at last, 'This won't be covered by the National Health

Service. It's only meant for people. I'm afraid you'll have to pay the full fee for this visit yourself, Mrs Barker.'

The woman made a wry face. 'I suppose you wouldn't like to have a kitten by way of payment, Nurse? This lot will be ready to go in a few weeks,' she said hopefully.

* * *

Going back the way she had come, Maudie travelled more slowly than before. As she contemplated what had just happened, her thoughts ranged all the way from fury to indignation. Suddenly the whole farcical experience struck her as funny and she burst into loud laughter, howling until the tears ran down her face.

'Something got you in the funny bone, Nurse?'

A farm labourer, busily mending a fence in a field full of cattle, grinned at her from the other side of the ditch.

'Oh, hello, Seth! I was just thinking about a joke someone told me this

113

morning, that's all.'

'Must have been a good one, then. Going to share it with us, are you?'

'Sorry, it's a bit private. But yes, it was amusing, in a way. In fact, I'd say it was enough to make a cat laugh!'

By the time she reached her next patient of the day, Maudie had calmed down. After all, she reasoned, it was always better to be called out on a false alarm than to arrive on the scene too late — at least, where human patients were concerned!

14

That evening she called on the vicar. She found him sitting next to the kitchen range wearing a shabby old Jaeger dressing gown and a pair of leather slippers. After she had taken his temperature, pulse and blood pressure, she pronounced herself satisfied.

'Early bed for you tonight, though, Mr Blunt, don't you think?'

He grunted. 'I've had enough of bed, Nurse! They were very kind at the hospital but I've never been one for lying around in the daytime, you know.'

Joan Blunt entered the room with Perkin at her heels. The cat stared at Maudie balefully. She reached out to pat him and he turned and fled, growling. Mrs Blunt laughed. 'Don't mind him, Nurse. He's just a bit disgruntled because we've been away.'

'Welcome to the club,' her husband muttered. 'I didn't ask to be sent to hospital, you know.'

'Just what were you up to, out on the road at that time of night?' Maudie asked. 'Had you been called to a sick parishioner?'

'The police keep asking me that, and no, I wasn't. I'd overdone it at dinner, eating one too many dumplings with Joan's stew. It seemed to be lying heavily on my stomach — no reflection on your excellent cooking, my dear — so I thought I'd have a little meander up the road before I locked up for the night. Joan had already gone up, so I just slipped out, only meaning to be gone five minutes. I told myself I'd go to the end of the street and turn back, but I'm told that I never made it that far.'

'Did you hear the vehicle coming? Was it travelling too fast?'

The vicar put up a hand to scratch his forehead. 'I can't remember. It's all a blank. I remember leaving the house, but that's all, until I woke up in hospital. I do wish the police would stop harping on about it. It was just an accident. I was wearing my dark overcoat, and the driver didn't see me until it was too late. That's all it was. I've always said that we need street lamps here in Llandyfan, and now perhaps the council will take sit up and take notice.'

'It may have been an accident,' Maudie said sternly, 'but to keep going, leaving a pedestrian for dead, is quite reprehensible. What if you had died? He'd have been charged with manslaughter then.'

'And you could have died if Nurse hadn't found you and taken charge as she did. Isn't there something you'd like to say to her, dear?'

Maudie hid a smile. Her friend's admonition reminded her of a small boy leaving a party, being encouraged by his mother to say, 'Thank you for my nice tea.'

The vicar nodded. 'I'm most grateful, Nurse. Had it not been for you I might be in my grave by now.'

'Of course, the police say it may have been a deliberate attack,' Mrs Blunt went on. 'Because of those beastly letters, you see. But I don't see how that could be. Harold went out on the spur of the moment. How could anyone know that he'd do that? It's not as if he made a habit of going out for a stroll last thing at night.'

'Have you any idea who could be sending those letters?' Maudie asked.

The vicar shook his head. 'I've thought and thought, but nothing springs to mind. The latest one calls me a murderer, but I've never caused the death of anybody, as far as I know. And I don't think we know anybody in London, unless you count Joan's old Auntie Vera, and she's safely tucked up in an old folks' home in Maida Vale!'

Auntie Vera couldn't be completely ruled out, Maudie thought when she was on her way home, keeping a wary eye out for death-dealing motorists. Oh, the old lady couldn't have been behind the wheel of the car that hit the vicar, and neither was she likely to have taken out a contract to have someone else kill the poor man.

She might be writing the poison-pen letters, though. As a nurse, Maudie was well aware that perfectly decent people could come up with some far-fetched notions after they became senile. She remembered one very respectable Baptist minister who used the most foul language when dealing with the nursing staff. She was convinced that he would never have behaved in such a manner had he been in his right mind. It was almost as if strait-laced people avoided any nastiness in their daily lives by keeping it all bottled up, and then it spilled over when their minds gave way in old age.

So, then, Auntie could be sitting in her room at the home, whiling away the boring hours by penning nasty little missives. It would be easy enough to hand the finished product to a care assistant to post.

All this brought Maudie no nearer to a solution as to what had happened to the vicar. It was maddening not to know the truth of the matter, and she said as much to Dick, when he phoned her at bedtime. He had taken to calling her just to say good night, which was sweet of him.

'Oh, I expect we'll get to the bottom of it soon,' he said.

'But what is being done? Are you

allowed to tell me?'

'Oh, it's no big secret. We've got men checking all the garages in the area to see if anyone has brought a vehicle in for repairs lately. We found pieces of glass on the road where the vicar was struck down, so there must be a damaged headlamp at least.'

'But the letters. What are the chances there?'

'That's in the hand of the Metropolitan Police now. It's just possible that Mr Blunt isn't the only one receiving these things. Sooner or later the man will slip up.'

'Man?'

'Or woman. What else have you been up to since I spoke to you last?'

'I went over to Midvale to do a bit of shopping. I hoped I might catch a glimpse of you but I didn't like to call at the station. I know how your chief feels about you getting personal calls at work. Anyway, I went out to see Miss Mallory, the old doc's sister, and what do you think?'

'She's got that youngster working for

her, Wilfred Fletcher.'

'Aw! How do you know?'

'Because I looked into it as soon as you reported to me what he said to you at the funeral. We can't have con men preying on old ladies.'

'And is he a con man?'

'Not as far as we know, but we're keeping our eyes open in case. It appears that he spent his youth in a series of foster homes, and since then he's had one or two menial jobs before turning up here. He's had no convictions of any kind, so I assume he's just one of nature's unfortunates.'

'What about his parents?'

'Who knows? Killed during the war, perhaps?'

'But aren't you going to find out?'

Dick sighed. 'We just don't have the manpower, Maudie. We've other things to think about: the attack on Mr Blunt, for instance. Unless this Wilfred puts a foot wrong we've no reason to take this any further.'

'But why would the lad claim to be Dr Mallory's son?'

'Surely you studied psychology as a student nurse, Maudie? I understand it's quite a common thing for an orphan to fantasise about who his parents were. We all want to belong somewhere, don't we? Plenty of people would like to claim a father such as Dr Mallory — kindly, well thought of in the community. And the best part, as far as young Wilfred is concerned, is that the old boy is dead and can't refute his claims. It's harmless, Maudie. I don't think we need to worry about it. Now listen, there go the pips, and I've no more change. Night-night, my love. Sleep tight.'

But Maudie did worry about it. Oh, probably the police were right, and the boy meant no harm to Miss Mallory. At least, she hoped so. But what if it was true, and Wilfred really was the doctor's son? She considered the facts.

Wilfred seemed to be in his early twenties. Dr Mallory had been in his eighties when he died. So if he had fathered the boy he would have been sixty-odd at the time. Quite possible biologically, she supposed.

Where had the doctor been between the wars? As far as she knew he had been practising at Midvale, even that long ago. So who would the boy's mother have been? Surely she couldn't have been a local girl. In a place the size of Midvale everyone would have known if their popular doctor was keeping company with a young woman, especially one who was probably half his age. Yet if there had been a secret liaison, news of that would have leaked out eventually because that was how things were in a small town.

Maudie had been introduced to Charlotte Brontë's novel *Jane Eyre* at school and had re-read it several times since. What if the poor doctor had married a woman who had gone mad — not as a result of being married to him, of course — and that was a dark secret? Not that she'd be hidden away in the attic like Mrs Rochester, but she could be in an asylum. The woman would have given birth in the late nineteen-twenties, when medical science was less advanced than it was now. Perhaps she had suffered from post-partum depression, and had been wrongly diagnosed and locked away? Why, she might be there still!

'Oh, do pull yourself together, Maudie Rouse!' she said crossly, speaking aloud. 'This is Llandyfan in the year 1950. You're not in the middle of a Gothic novel! Pull yourself together, you idiot, and go to bed.'

She did turn in for the night after carefully laying out her clean clothes for the morning, but somehow the little puzzle continued to niggle at her in the following days. Maudie did so like to have everything cut and dried.

15

On the following Saturday afternoon something happened to drive all thoughts of Dr Mallory's mythical son out of her mind. She was expecting Dick to come for his tea and, as it would be their last evening together before he left for Hendon, she wanted the meal to be special. Shepherd's pie was hardly gourmet fare, but she meant to spice it up a little with the addition of cauliflower au gratin and a new brand of chutney she'd been wanting to sample. She would put a dollop of that into a little glass dish a patient had given her at Christmas; she did want the table to look pretty.

After much struggling and muttering, when the lid of the chutney jar refused to budge she held it under the hot-water tap, still without success. She might have to resort to her old trick of driving a nail into the lid with the hammer, thus releasing the pressure. The problem with that was that the lid would no longer be airtight and the contents might go mouldy in the larder.

The doorbell rang. Maudie went to answer the door, still clutching the jar.

'Dr Ransome! What a surprise!'

'May I come in, Nurse?'

'Of course. Do come through to the kitchen; I've got potatoes on the stove and I don't want them boiling over. Please excuse the mess. I'm expecting company for tea.'

'Don't worry, Nurse. I won't stop long. I was just passing and I thought I'd drop in to say hello. There wasn't time to say much to each other at the reception, but I'm sure we shall enjoy working together once we get to know each other.'

Maudie struggled with the chutney jar again to cover her confusion. What on earth was the man playing at? They had been practically engaged until he had thrown her over in favour of that society beauty. Was he going to pretend that they were strangers to each other?

'Here, let me,' he said, taking the jar from Maudie in his left hand. He made

126

one deft movement with the other hand and the lid came off with a satisfying pop.

She looked up at him. Gazed into his tawny brown eyes. Her heart quickened its pace and she had to wait for a moment until it settled down again.

'Anything wrong, Nurse?'

Maudie bit her lip. 'No, no, Dr Ransome. Seeing you getting that lid off so easily for me reminded me about a patient, Mrs Fleming. She has bad arthritis, you know, and she can't manage things like bottle tops. Well, I promised her ages ago that I'd take her some magazines I've finished with, and I've completely forgotten all about it. What must she be thinking of me!'

The doctor looked at her quizzically, but he seemed to accept her explanation and they chatted amiably until he left, saying that he'd see her on Monday at the surgery.

She leaned against the door when he had gone, her mind racing. He must have thought she was a blithering idiot. But that didn't matter, as long as he didn't know what she was really thinking.

The Julian Ransome she had known was left-handed. She had watched him lovingly so many times when she was on night duty and he was sitting beside her, making notations on patients' charts. He had worn his expensive watch on his right wrist. She knew that Julian had served in the war and that many men had learned to use a different hand after being wounded. But there was nothing wrong with either one of this man's hands. He had proved that by opening her jar of chutney with effortless ease.

And she had almost fainted when she'd looked into those brown eyes, because she had spent so many hours gazing adoringly into her Julian's eyes — his blue eyes — as he told her how much he loved her.

There could possibly be some rational explanation for his dexterity, although she couldn't imagine what it might be. But his eyes were another matter. Maudie knew that for centuries inventors had been trying to develop lenses that could be worn next to the eyes. She had read an article in a magazine that described the invention of a plastic lens by a man in

California as recently as two years ago. She seemed to remember that they were called contact lenses. But they were clear, weren't they? Surely they couldn't make blue eyes turn brown?

Something just wasn't right about this Julian Ransome. He looked very much like the Julian she had known; greyer around the temples, yes, but that was only to be expected when she hadn't seen him for a number of years. And his experience as a doctor at war, treating men with horrible injuries, must have been enough to turn a saint grey.

And if this was a different man it would explain why he was behaving as if they'd never met before. But if he wasn't her former love, then who on earth could he be? She knew that Julian didn't have a brother, and of course a sibling would have had a different name in any case. Nor could she recall hearing of any cousin who might resemble him. Maudie could distinctly remember being told that his parents were very proud of the fact that he was the first man in their family ever to qualify as a doctor.

They say that we all have a look-alike somewhere in the world: a double. Therefore there might be umpteen men who closely resembled Julian. But what were the odds against two identical men, with a similar name, being doctors?

Twins, of course! She had read stories of twins separated at birth who quite independently followed a parallel path, perhaps following the same career, both marrying spouses with similar names or appearance, even getting wed on the same day.

Come on, Maudie, she admonished herself. *You know it's a possibility!* In her time she had delivered babies for quite a few unmarried mothers who had been forced to give them up because that was what society demanded. A child born out of wedlock was often punished for its mother's 'sin' and it was thought best to save a child from that. And very often the mothers were too young to be able to support themselves properly, let alone a baby.

But Julian had certainly not told her he'd been adopted, and if that had been the case it was something he should have shared with his prospective bride, as he had led Maudie to believe she was. They were both trained in the medical field and they were aware that certain conditions were hereditary. Sadly, adopted children rarely knew anything about such diseases in their bloodlines, so they were left in the dark when it came to producing their own children.

There again, it was always possible that his adoptive parents hadn't told him about his origins, preferring to let him think that he was their biological child.

Maudie paused, her thoughts returning to the possibility that the two Julians were twins. 'I am such a fool,' she said aloud. The two men had different eye colours, so they could not be identical twins, could they? And could fraternal twins resemble each other as closely as these two did?

Well, there was only one way to get to the bottom of this puzzle, and that was to trace the Dr Julian Ransome she used to know. She could start by writing to their old training hospital, asking for his current address. If for some reason they were reluctant to give it to her, she could say that she was an old friend (true) who wanted to invite him to her forthcoming wedding (not on your life).

In the meantime she would do her best to collect a little dossier on this new Dr Ransome. It wouldn't hurt to ask him a few general questions under the guise of showing a welcoming interest. Where was he from? Mrs Hatch had mentioned Gloucestershire.

Where had he trained? Surely it was reasonable to ask about that. In fact, she would take a good look around the surgery in the morning. Most doctors liked to display framed copies of their professional certificates where the patients could see them. That information would give her a head start.

Much later Maudie was to ask herself why she hadn't come right out at the reception and mentioned that she had known another Dr Julian Ransome — something that any normal person would have done. But hindsight is a wonderful thing, and Maudie had no more ability to see into the future than anybody else.

16

'Morning, Nurse! I hope you don't mind my dropping in this early. Only, I wanted to catch you before you left for the surgery.'

'Not at all, Mrs Black. Is it about young Frankie?'

'Oh, no; he's all right. A bit fractious at the moment, mind, on account of he's cutting teeth. No, I wanted a word with you about something else entirely.'

Maudie thought she knew what was coming 'You want me to talk to Matt, I suppose. Well, I don't know that I should interfere. People only do what they want to do in the end, you know, and then who gets the blame when it all goes wrong?'

Some months earlier Maudie had been caught in the middle of their family squabble. Mrs Black's daughter Greta, aged seventeen, had become pregnant by nineteen-year-old Matt Flynn, an apprentice mechanic. Greta's father had insisted that the baby must be given up for adoption, but the young couple had set out to drive to Gretna Green, meaning to get married there.

Before long Greta's pains had started and they'd turned round to return to Llandyfan, but the car had slid off the road and Maudie had been forced to deliver the baby in the back seat of the vehicle. Fortunately mother and child came through the ordeal safely, and in the aftermath Frank Black had changed his mind and allowed his daughter to keep the baby.

'Which I think now was a mistake,' her mother concluded when Maudie reminisced about this. 'Mind you, the baby is a lovely little chap, and I wouldn't have wanted to lose my only grandchild, but Greta takes no more notice of him than if he was a pet kitten. She lolls about with her head in those film magazines of hers, and leaves everything to me. The dirty nappies pile up and I'm forced to deal with them. I don't possess a washing machine and I have to do it all by hand, scrubbing them on a washboard and then boiling them in a bucket on the stove. It's more than I bargained for at my age, Nurse, I can tell you that!'

'You'll just have to be firm with her, Mrs Black. She's a mother now and she must take responsibility for everything to do with that baby. Personally I think she's a very lucky girl to be still living under your roof, with your hubby footing the bill for everything.'

'I'm afraid to say too much in case she runs off with Matt again, leaving little Frankie on my hands,' Mrs Black muttered, wiping the corner of her eye with the end of her woolly scarf.

'Really? I thought that was all over.' Matt had been acting the big man in front of his friends, bragging about fathering a son when some of them were still schoolboys. His enhanced status had drawn the local girls to him like wasps to a honey pot and Greta, furious at his neglect of her, had given him his marching orders.

'Oh, it's all on again, up to a point, Nurse. The boy has fallen short on the maintenance he's supposed to pay for the baby, and my Frank has had to chase after him for that. It's only a pittance, mind, but it's the principle of the thing. And that Mrs Flynn has been coming around, demanding what she calls her grandmother's rights, and she's been nagging at her Matt to come with her when she visits. Frank says they should either get married like they planned before, or the Flynns should keep their distance so Greta's free to meet someone decent. That's got her back up, of course, so she's encouraging Matt to make up to her again.'

'Yes, well, Mrs Black, this is all very interesting and I'm so sorry to hear you're having a hard time, but I really mustn't get involved. I'm a midwife, not a social worker. And now, if you'll excuse me, I really must get started. I'm expected at the surgery this morning, and after that I have a list of home visits to do.' Maudie stood up, a signal to the woman that the interview was over.

Mrs Black looked over her shoulder, as if to make sure that she couldn't be overheard. 'I didn't come here to talk about my problems with Greta, Nurse. This is about Matt. I think he's the one who almost did for the vicar, and I don't know what I ought to do about it.'

'What!' Maudie sat down again in a hurry. 'Whatever makes you say a thing like that?'

'He's got this old car, see. It's an old rattletrap of a thing. His boss let him have it for next to nothing, seeing it's as old as the hills. According to Mrs Flynn the chap said it would give the lad something do in his spare time. If he could fix it up using the skills he was learning on the job, it would give him useful experience, see?'

'And?'

'Well, he arrived the other night looking a bit down in the mouth. Told us the brakes had gone and he'd crashed into a dry-stone wall. He asked if he could leave it in that derelict barn we have on the back of the farm, just until he had time to work on it, like. He didn't want his boss to know what had happened.'

I bet he didn't, Maudie thought. 'So

you gave him permission to use the barn?' she prompted.

'Well yes. I didn't think anything of it until we heard about the poor vicar. Then I took a walk over there and had a look at that car, and it certainly must have run into something. One of the lights is smashed and that bumper thing in the front is hanging off at one end.'

'Well, Mrs Black, as I see it you have only two options. Either you report this to the police and let them deal with it, or you speak to Matt and encourage him to confess. Let him know that unless he turns himself in you'll do it for him.'

'What, inform on a neighbour? Oh, no, I couldn't do that, Nurse!'

'Then I don't see what you expect me to do.'

'I thought you could slip a word in your fiancé's ear, on the quiet, like. I've heard that the coppers are all over the place, asking questions at the garages and junkyards. You tip them off that there's something interesting in our barn and it'll look like they've just come across it by accident.'

Maudie looked the woman straight in the eye. 'All right, I'll do it, but only so the Blunts can have peace of mind. And as for Matt Flynn, I hope they throw the book at him. Leaving the scene of an accident is a crime, but causing harm to someone and not bothering to get help for them is pretty beastly.'

'I know, Nurse, I know.'

'And if you ask me, your Greta is well rid of that young man, and I advise you to do everything you can to split them up. You may lose that bit of maintenance the boy pays for his son, but he won't be able to pay that in any case if he goes to prison.'

'Prison! I hope it doesn't go that far.'

'That will be for the police to decide, or the judge, if this comes to court.' Maudie stood up again and this time she managed to send Mrs Black on her way. She glanced at the clock. There wasn't time to call Dick now. It wouldn't do for her to turn up late on her first day in attendance at Dr Ransome's surgery.

* * *

The surgery was crammed with people. The doctor looked despairingly at Maudie. 'What do you make of that lot out there, Nurse? Is it always like this, or have we been hit by an epidemic of bubonic plague all of a sudden?'

Maudie laughed. 'By the look of things they're mostly people who didn't get to Cora Beasley's reception the other day. My guess is that most of them just want to size you up and decide whether you'll make the grade in Llandyfan.'

'Oh, dear!'

'You don't have a receptionist yet, so why don't I announce each patient in turn? I'll dig out their charts for you, and I can fill you in on the background to each case and the home circumstance of the patient.'

'It sounds to me as if you should be the doctor here, not me!'

'Oh, you'll soon get used to us here, Dr Ransome, and the patients will soon get used to you. They are a pleasant lot, on the whole. One or two chronic grumblers, of course, but every practice must have its share of those.' She looked around the

140

small consulting room, her eyes focusing on the calendar with its photograph of the Yorkshire Dales that was the only adornment on the otherwise bare walls. 'I see you haven't had time to put up your certificates and such yet, Doctor.' She pointed to the wall. 'Dr Lennox had his displayed right there. See, the nail is still there for you to use. I find that the patients do like to look at the doctor's credentials. It gives them confidence, I suppose. May I enquire where you took your training, Dr Ransome?'

'Mary and Martha's,' he said.

'And a very good hospital, too, I believe. Now, we really must get started before we have a riot on our hands, so I'll show in the first patient, shall I?'

Without waiting for an answer, she pulled the door open and looked into the waiting room. Maudie was very much aware of just how good a hospital Mary and Martha's was, for hadn't she trained there herself? But she didn't want Dr Ransome to know that, or he'd realise that she was on to him. And she was certainly on the scent of something now, because it was quite obvious that something wasn't right.

⋆　⋆　⋆

Maudie had some difficulty in tracking Dick down when she tried to contact him later in the day. She was looking forward to discussing the latest developments with him so she declined to speak to another officer, who most probably would have made a note of her report without comment.

On the third attempt she struck lucky. Dick came to the phone, panting slightly. 'Is anything wrong, Maudie? They told me you've called several times.'

'Oh, all is well with me, but you sound a bit breathless. You're not having any chest pain, are you?'

'No, of course not. I'm fit as a flea. I've just run all the way up two flights of stairs to take your call, that's all.'

'Good. Well, I wanted to let you know that if you people have a look in that old abandoned barn on Frank Black's place you'll find something to your advantage.'

'Oh? And what might that be?'

'An old banger that Matt Flynn's been fixing up. At least, it'll need a lot more fixing now, because I've heard it has a smashed headlamp and a few wobbly bits.'

'And you think it could be the vehicle we're looking for, in connection with the attack on the vicar? Who told you this?'

'Never you mind. Just go and see it before it gets moved on.'

'Right-ho. Thanks, old girl.'

$$\star \quad \star \quad \star$$

Having done her duty, Maudie went to put the kettle on. She resolved not to say anything to the Blunts; it would be up to the police to let them know that the car had been found, and, possibly, that the driver had been apprehended. But would this bring them any peace of mind? It was quite likely that the vicar's tumble had been purely an accident and not a premeditated attack. Matt may have been ripping along, travelling much too fast, as young male drivers are prone to do; he may even have had a drink or two before he got behind the wheel. But that did not explain the poison-pen letters, nor did it mean that the vicar was no longer under threat from whoever had sent them.

Maudie could think of no reason why the boy should have written such letters. And even if he had done so, how could he have managed to post them in London? And thinking of letters, after today's little bombshell she now had even more reason to look into the doctor's background.

She must contact her old hospital immediately. Not only would she make enquiries about the present whereabouts of Dr Julian Ransome, but she would also try to trace any of her old set who might be able to tell her what had become of him after the war. Where had he practised medicine, for example? He hadn't necessarily returned to Mary and Martha's.

17

Any thoughts of writing to her old hospital had to be set aside when Maudie received a frantic message from Dilys Pugh, delivered by a small boy on a scooter.

'That Mrs Poo says can you come at once, Nurse, cos there's something wrong with the baby,' he lisped.

'Thank you, dear. I'll go and have a look right away,' she told him, ignoring his outstretched paw. She heard him mumble something under his breath as he trundled off. 'Join the Wolf Cubs!' she called after him. 'They have to do a good deed every day, and they don't expect to get paid!' Refreshed by the little encounter, she collected her bag and set off for the Pughs' brick semi.

She hoped it was nothing serious. After spending a month in the Cottage Hospital, the baby boy had come home weighing in at a respectable five pounds.

Maudie had hoped that it would all be plain sailing from this point on, as the Pughs got to know this much-wanted little son.

Dilys opened the door. Her husband had probably left for work already. She had been crying, and there were black smudges on her face where her mascara had run.

'You sent for me, I believe?' Maudie said when the woman made no move to invite her in.

'Oh, yes. I asked little Timmy from next door to fetch you. He found you, then?'

This was no time to deliver a sarcastic rejoinder, so Maudie simply moved forward so that Dilys was forced to step aside and let her in. 'Where is the baby, Mrs Pugh? What is his name, by the way?'

'Roger. We call him Roger. Roger Anthony Pugh.'

'Very nice, too. May I see the baby, Mrs Pugh?'

'Oh, no, please don't disturb him! I've just got him down and if he wakes up again I'll go mad, I know I will.' Tears welled up in her pale blue eyes.

'What you need is a good strong cup of tea, my girl! Have you had breakfast yet?'

'Er, no. I haven't had time.'

Right, then — you put your feet up on that sofa there and I'll make you some tea and toast.'

'But you can't. You don't know where everything is.'

'I'm sure I can find my way around your kitchen,' Maudie told her firmly. 'Now you just do as you're told and we'll soon have you feeling much better.'

Sure enough, her patient did appear much brighter after she had ingested two cups of strong tea and three rounds of toast and jam.

'There you are, you see,' Maudie told her. 'All you needed was a bit of something inside you. Caring for a small baby takes a lot out of a mother, you know. You must look after yourself, my dear. It won't help your Roger if his mother's health fails.'

'I know, I know. But I'm so tired all the time, Nurse! Just exhausted. I'm supposed to feed the baby every three hours, you see, but he's so slow and he takes forever to finish the bottle. He falls asleep when he's supposed to be feeding, but as soon as I put him down he starts to wail. I'm so desperate for sleep, Nurse. I just don't know how I can carry on!'

'Believe me, I do understand, Mrs Pugh. Most babies suck instinctively but Roger was born prematurely, as of course you know, and he had to be fed through a tube at the hospital. He has to learn how to take a bottle now. He'll buck up soon enough and then you'll be able to establish a better routine. In the meantime we have to do something to help you. I suggest that you let your husband take over at the weekend while you get some much-needed rest. Better still, get out for an hour or two. Take the bus to Midvale and have a look round the shops.'

'Oh, Ray wouldn't do that! Looking after babies is women's work, that's what he'd say if I even suggested it.'

'And I suppose all the cooking and washing and ironing is women's work, too?'

'Yes, of course it is. I don't know what

you mean, Nurse!'

'What I mean is that you're expected to do all the work of the household and care for a premature baby as well, aren't you?'

Dilys Pugh still looked puzzled. 'But that's what marriage is all about, isn't it? The man goes out and earns a living for his family and in return he expects to find a clean and comfortable home waiting for him and his dinner on the table. I can't expect Ray to come home tired out after a hard day at the office and start looking after babies.'

She was right, of course — up to a point. That had always been the traditional outlook, but the war had brought changes with it. Years ago, in villages like Llandyfan, a young mother could count on help from her mother and sisters, who probably lived in the same district. Nowadays, when people moved into other communities in order for the men to find jobs, women such as Dilys Pugh had become isolated, and there wasn't a great deal that Maudie could do to alleviate the problem.

A thin wail came from an inner room.

Mrs Pugh struggled to her feet. 'There, what did I tell you? He's off again.'

'I'll see to him this time,' Maudie said. 'You can lie down on that sofa and have forty winks. I'll go and change the baby while you heat up his bottle.'

Soon Maudie was sitting contentedly in an armchair, feeding the tiny infant. He was so small and helpless, having been born too soon. If hospital treatment had not been available to him his survival could have been in doubt, or he might at least have been left with developmental problems.

Her mind drifted to the faraway Mrs Dionne, mother of the famous quintuplets. The doctor who had assisted with the birth had taken charge of the situation. The girls had been removed from their parents' home and a small hospital was built nearby in which to raise the little girls. How had this affected their poor mother?

Dilys Pugh had been under stress while baby Roger was in hospital. She hadn't been allowed to hold him, nor even to visit him, and the enforced separation had been almost like a death at the time. In fact, as she confided to Maudie, she hadn't known whether to hope for a happy outcome or to distance herself from her baby in her mind, in case the worst happened.

Surely the young French-Canadian mother must have experienced similar anguish? But on the other hand, how could she possibly have looked after five tiny infants that needed specialised care? Maudie acknowledged that she herself, despite being a trained nurse and a midwife, would not have been able to cope if left alone in such a situation, all round the clock.

Since receiving Dick's Christmas gift Maudie had taken a renewed interest in the Dionne case, going so far as to dig out a scrapbook she'd made of their story before the war. Elzire Dionne had given birth to fourteen children by the time she was thirty, having married at the age of fifteen. Maudie's own grandma had produced fourteen children, which was very much the norm in Queen Victoria's day — but she hadn't even had twins, let alone quintuplets!

Little Roger had stopped suckling and seemed to be sound asleep. Maudie was on the point of drifting off herself. She noticed that the baby had taken less than an ounce of milk, and time was passing. She gently flicked a finger on the sole of one his miniature bare feet and he started awake, thrusting out his arms in a sudden reflex.

When at long last the baby had taken in as much of his feed as she could persuade him to swallow, Maudie burped him and changed his nappy. 'In one end, out the other!' she told him lovingly as she inserted the safety pins, making sure that they were properly fastened. The baby immediately soaked himself and she had to go through the whole process again.

'You little rascal!' she told him. 'Nothing but trouble, that's what you are!' She didn't mean it, of course, but she was happy enough to settle him in his cot before tiptoeing out of the room. She had done her bit, and thankfully she did not have to get up in the wee hours of the morning to feed him again.

He slept. In the living room his weary mother dozed on. Maudie yawned and went out into the cold morning, pulling the door to behind her. A frigid wind made her face smart. She longed to return home and crawl back into her own cosy bed, but duty called.

18

Maudie had meant to write a letter to her old hospital, but after screwing up three sheets of good note paper, dissatisfied with what she'd written, she decided to telephone instead.

Having got through to the busy personnel department, she came straight to the point. 'Hello, this is Nurse Maudie Rouse. I did my training at Mary and Martha's.'

'How can I help you?'

'Well, you see, I'm about to get married and . . .'

'Congratulations!'

'Thank you. The thing is, I want to invite some of my old chums to the wedding, and I can't seem to find Dr Julian Ransome. I suppose you wouldn't happen to know where he is now?'

The person on the other end of the line cleared her throat. 'I'm sorry, the name doesn't ring a bell. But then I've only been here two years. When did you say you graduated?'

'I didn't say, but we both left there when the war started. I know that Julian joined up, but I don't know where he went after the war ended.'

'I don't think he came back here, Nurse. At least, there's nobody of that name on the staff now.'

Maudie thought for a moment. 'I'm pretty sure there must be an association of doctors who were medical students there. I remember them holding old boys' reunions, or whatever they might have called doctors who trained there.'

'Ah, you want Dr Phillipson, then. He's the current head of the Graduates' Association. Shall I connect you?'

'Yes, please.'

Maudie had to wait quite some time for the doctor to come to the phone, and meanwhile the minutes were ticking away and her hard-earned cash with them! She was about to hang up when a loud voice sounded in her ear, causing her to hold the earpiece away from her head.

'Phillipson!'

'Good morning, Doctor. I'm trying to learn the current whereabouts of Dr Julian Ransome, who was at Mary and Martha's before the war. Would you happen to know where he's working at the moment?'

'And who might you be?'

'My name is Rouse. I knew him when I was working at your hospital and I want to invite him to my wedding, only we seem to have lost touch.'

'Hang on a sec while I dig out the register.'

A metallic clanking told Maudie that he was probably searching a filing cabinet of sorts. Then she heard his returning footsteps and the phone was picked up again.

'Yes, here we are, miss. Julian Ransome, qualified 1937. And according to my records he's currently a member of a practice in some place in the back of beyond called Llandyfan.'

'Llandyfan! Are you sure?'

'That's what it says here. Now, is there anything else? I'm a busy man and I've no time to waste chatting about the geography of the British Isles.'

'Thank you for your time, Doctor.'

Thoughtfully, Maudie replaced the receiver. She was no further ahead than when she'd started. Perhaps she needed to talk to another woman who had known Julian. Women were so much better at absorbing little details about the people they knew.

She redialed the number of the hospital and was put through to the personnel department again. This time she drew a different clerk who was much more knowledgeable.

'This is Nurse Maudie Rouse. I did my training there before the war. I'm getting married now and I'd love to have some of my old set at my wedding.'

'How lovely!'

'Thank you. The thing is, I don't know how to find most of them anymore. Oh, you know how it is — we all swore to keep in touch, but then the war intervened and that put paid to all our good intentions.'

'Tell me about it! So you want to know

if any of your old mates are still working here, is that right?'

'Yes, please. The 1938 set.'

'I suppose you could ask Sister Martin in Male Surgical. She's been here since the year dot. She might know something.'

'I don't recall a nurse by that name.'

'You might have known her as Doris Perry. I'm told she left here to get married right after earning her State registration, but her hubby was killed in the war and she came back to work. Been here ever since.'

'Why, yes! I remember her! A tall girl with red hair.'

'That's right. Listen. Why don't I call her ward? She must be just about to go off duty. We'll catch her if we're quick.'

'Sister Martin speaking.'

'Doris! Is that you? Maudie Rouse here.'

'Rouse! I can't believe it! The last time I heard of you, you were off to do your midder. Are you in town? Do you want to get together for a coffee and catch up on all our news?'

'No,' Maudie said. 'I'm at home, and

this is a trunk call. But I would like to pick your brains about something, if that's all right.'

'Of course. Anything I can do to help.'

Maudie chose her words with care. She didn't want to let slip that she was actually living in the same community as Julian Ransome, or Sister Martin would wonder what she was up to.

'Do you happen to remember Julian Ransome? He was a houseman at Mary and Martha's when we were in our third year.'

'Julian Ransome! Well of course I remember him. We all thought you two might make a go of it, until he threw you over in favour of that blonde with all the money.'

Maudie winced. 'Obviously it wasn't meant to be, which is just as well because I'm engaged to a lovely chap now, and we're planning our wedding. I want to invite Julian to the do, just so he can see what he's missing!' She chuckled, trying to make her story sound convincing.

There was a long pause, and then Sister Martin told Maudie something that she hadn't expected to hear. 'I'm afraid that you won't be able to get your revenge at your wedding, Rouse. Julian Ransome is dead.'

'Dead!' Maudie squeaked. 'That's not right! He can't be dead!'

'Yes, I think so.'

'But how? When?'

'In North Africa during the war.'

'How do you know?'

'My Bob told me,' Sister Martin said, with a catch in her voice. 'That is to say, he mentioned it in one of his letters home.'

'Do you recall what he said, Doris?'

Again Maudie heard that little catch in the other woman's voice. 'Not exactly. I suppose it wasn't long after that when Bob was killed and everything seemed like a blur for a long while.'

'I quite understand.'

'I've kept all his letters to me, meaning to go over them some day, but I haven't quite plucked up the courage yet.'

'These things take time,' Maudie murmured.

'They do indeed, but life must go on. I

get the feeling that there's more to this than just a wedding invitation, Rouse. Am I right?'

'Well, I would like to know what happened to Julian,' Maudie answered, feeling like a complete fraud. The other nurse was still grieving for a lost husband, and here was Maudie, trying to pull the wool over her eyes.

Sister Martin seemed to come to a decision. 'Look here, I'll have a look at Bob's letters and let you know what he said about Julian, okay?'

'Well, if it's not too painful for you.'

'Not to worry. I'll have to deal with it sometime. It might as well be now. Give me your details and then I'd better hang up. Your phone bill is going to be the size of Mount Everest!'

19

'Where would you like to go on your honeymoon?' Dick asked. 'That is, I mean our honeymoon.' He laughed self-consciously.

Maudie looked at him, pleased. 'Oh, I don't know. I suppose somewhere nice and quiet with pretty scenery. The Lake District, perhaps? Or Scotland?'

'I'd love to see both those places some day, but how about abroad?'

She paused in her knitting to frown at him in a friendly fashion. 'I've already said I don't want to emigrate, Dick.'

'Oh, I know we're not going to Canada, old girl. But how about France?'

Paris, she thought. Yes — the most romantic city in the world! Of course the country had just come through a war, and no doubt Paris had taken a bit of a bashing from Hitler's troops, but there would still be plenty to see.

She began to dream. There was the

Eiffel Tower, of course — probably one of the best-known landmarks in the world. There was the Louvre, which had once been a palace belonging to French royalty and was now home to fabulous art treasures, if they had survived the war.

She could imagine herself — with Dick, of course — strolling down the Champs-Elysées, or gazing in admiration at the Arc de Triomphe, that stunning piece of architecture commissioned by the Emperor Napoleon to celebrate his victory at Austerlitz. And there might be tour boats travelling on the Seine, too; it would be fun to ride in one of those. And what about the dress shops and the fashion houses! Everyone knew that Paris was the fashion capital of the world. She could never afford to patronise a couturier, of course, but window-shopping cost nothing, and she could always buy a pretty scarf or a tiny bottle of perfume as a souvenir of the holiday.

'Yoo-hoo! Anybody home?'

'I was only thinking,' Maudie said, laughing. 'Paris, here I come!'

The tips of Dick's ears turned pink. 'Um, I was thinking more of visiting some of the battlegrounds,' he said. 'I'd like to show you the places where I served with the army during the war. I'd get a better idea of what we were up against if I had a good look round in peacetime, you see. When you're in the thick of it all you don't know what's going on right next door to you.'

'Right.' Maudie raised her eyes to the ceiling but he didn't notice anything amiss.

'And while I'm at it I should visit a couple of the places where they're setting up cemeteries, to see what sort of progress they're making. I lost a number of good mates over there and I'd like to think they haven't been forgotten.'

Maudie cleared her throat. 'Dick. Dear Dick. Your ideas are very commendable, I'm sure, but do you really think we should spend our honeymoon travelling down a not-very-happy memory lane? Visit the battlegrounds by all means, at some other time. Let's go to France and enjoy ourselves.'

He looked disappointed for a moment, but at last he nodded in agreement.

'I suppose we'll cross the Channel by steamer,' Maudie said, hoping to strike while the iron was hot. 'And what will we do when we get there? Hire a car?'

Dick beamed. 'No, I thought we'd take a tandem. We'd see a lot more of the country that way. I know a bloke who'll sell me one cheap.'

Maudie dropped a stitch. If France was anything like England she could just see herself pedalling along for miles with the rain pelting down on her bowed head, and her only view being that of Dick's back, clad in oilskins.

He threw back his head and roared with laughter. 'If you could see your face, Maudie! I was just kidding of course. What I really have in mind is to get a sidecar fitted onto the motorbike and you can travel in state.'

She wasn't sure if he was still joking, but one thing she knew for sure: she was not about to spend her holiday of a lifetime squashed into a sidecar while Dick leaned over the handlebars looking like the Red Baron in a helmet and goggles.

'I know!' she said, hunting in her knitting bag for a crochet hook so she could retrieve the dropped stitch before any further damage was done. 'We'll pop across the Channel and then I'll go to Paris and you can go and look at the ruins of Caen. That way we'll both be satisfied.'

'You're serious, aren't you?' Dick asked.

'I am. Very.'

'All right, old girl. Let's leave it for a bit and see what else we can come up with that suits us both.'

She beamed at him. It said a lot for Dick's temperament that he was willing to listen to her point of view. What must it be like to live with someone like Raymond Pugh, whose word was law?

'By the way,' Dick said, 'I meant to tell you, there's been a development in the case of the attack on the vicar.'

'Oh, yes?'

'Our boys paid a visit to that derelict barn, and low and behold, there was the car, just as you said. I don't know how you knew it was there, but Maudie Marple strikes again!'

'And are they sure they've got the right vehicle, the one that knocked Mr Blunt down?'

'Oh yes, it's a match all right. Of course Frank Black denies all knowledge of the thing. He says he hasn't been inside that building in a month of Sundays, and he doesn't recognise the vehicle.'

'He won't get into trouble over it, will he?'

'Hard to say. He could just be an innocent bystander.'

'Was it a stolen car, then?' Knowing full well that it wasn't, Maudie couldn't resist putting Dick on the spot. There were times when he withheld information from her, on the grounds that it was police business, and she was only a member of the public who did not have the right to know everything that was going on in his world.

'Oh no, it's been traced to a chap living over at Brookfield, but he says he sold it to a garage here in Llandyfan, more or less for scrap. And guess who has been monkeying about with it, trying to fix it up for his own use?'

'Matt Flynn.'

'You knew all the time, didn't you?'

'Not really. Anybody could have been driving it that night. It could even have been stolen from Matt, or sold to another fellow by him.'

'It was Matt driving, right enough. When we got hold of him he confessed right away. We didn't even need to take him down to the nick before he started to squeal, although we had to escort him there after he'd been charged with reckless driving and leaving the scene.'

'So what's his story?'

Dick shrugged. 'Just what you might expect. The brakes were soft and he couldn't stop in time. He thought he might have hit a dog or something, but he wasn't sure. He had to get home because his mother worries if he stops out late.'

'A likely story. Well, she'll be worried now, won't she?' Maudie shook her head in disbelief. 'We know it was dark that night, and by his own admission the vicar was wearing dark clothing, but what sort of person thinks they hit a dog and fails to stop and see what they can do to help it?'

'The likes of Matt Flynn, obviously.'

Maudie folded her knitting and crammed it into her bag. 'So what happens next?'

'I understand that the vicar has decided to set a Christian example by not pressing charges against the boy.'

Maudie shrugged. 'That sounds like Harold Blunt, all right. But what about the threatening letters? He's not out of the woods yet, even though we know he wasn't run down on purpose.'

20

Maudie's tea-towels were a disgrace. Two of them were frayed at the edges and threadbare. One more wash would finish them off, and they were only fit for the ragbag as it was. Clothing and other material goods had been strictly rationed during the war, and she had preferred to use her meagre allowance of clothing coupons to replace underclothes and stockings.

The system had been abolished some months earlier, although that didn't mean that you could always find what you wanted in the shops. She set out for Midvale with hope in her heart.

In Bentham's department store she climbed to the second floor and examined the goods on offer. The only tea-towels on display were some very shoddy items in a red-and-white check. Wrinkling the cloth between her fingers and thumb, she eyed it with distaste. That red dye would probably run all over the place the first time she washed it.

Where had all the nice Irish linen cloths gone? They were being sold in America probably. A couple of years ago she had spotted a very pretty rose-patterned china teapot in this very store, locked up in a glass-fronted cabinet and bearing a label saying 'for export only'. What on earth was the point of that? Many a woman would have given her eyeteeth to be able to purchase such a thing after the years of shortages, and this was rubbing their noses in it with a vengeance.

Was there some government department charged with the job of sending out unobtainable goods as a way to show consumers that British industry was getting back on its feet after the war? If that was the case they had a funny way of showing it.

These towels just wouldn't do. Maudie decided to wander up to the fabric department and see if they had anything suitable there. It wouldn't take her long to hem a couple of remnants.

As she turned to go she noticed a man frowning over the goods on offer. He, too, picked up a towel and put it down again, obviously unimpressed.

'Good morning, Mr Pugh.'

He looked up, blinking. 'Oh, er, good morning, Nurse.'

'How are your wife and little Roger?'

'Quite well, I think.'

'And Mrs Pugh has sent you shopping, has she? Can I be of help at all? All the assistants seem to have gone on strike.'

'Perhaps you can advise me,' he said. 'I'm looking for something for my wife's birthday, you see. It's coming up in a couple of days.'

Maudie warmed to the man as she hadn't done previously. He had remembered his wife's birthday! More than that, he was trying to buy her a present! That was more than you could say for a lot of husbands. She gave him her best smile. 'And what are you going to buy her?'

'That's my problem. How do I know what she wants?'

'It shouldn't be too difficult to find out, surely?'

'You don't know my wife, Nurse. I bought her a very nice electric iron for Christmas, and when she unwrapped it she burst into tears. I know women get emotional when they're in the family way but that was uncalled for. I thought she'd be able to iron my shirts much more quickly if she didn't have to keep heating those flat irons on the hob.'

Maudie managed to suppress a sigh. 'I agree with you that labour-saving devices are welcome in the general way of things, Mr Pugh. In fact a cousin of mine sent me a bodkin for Christmas and I was very pleased to get it. It's been years since I've seen one in the shops.' She leaned closer to him, tapping her nose. 'I'll let you in on a little secret about women, shall I, Mr Pugh?'

'Please do,' he said, glancing over his shoulder to make sure they weren't being overheard. Who knew what ghastly piece of information a nurse might have to impart!

'We ladies like to get something personal when it comes to Christmas and birthday gifts. Something to show that the giver cares.'

'Personal! You surely don't mean underwear, Nurse! I couldn't possibly go into the ladieswear department and look at things there. People might think there was something wrong with me.'

'I wasn't thinking of lingerie, Mr Pugh. What about a pretty scarf, for instance?'

'She's got a woollen one with gloves to match.'

'I meant something she could wear for a special occasion, to brighten up a plain frock. Or perhaps she'd like a head square, to wear when she takes little Roger out in his pram? I see a pile of them on the next counter. Shall we go and look?' Maudie picked up a paisley-patterned square in attractive pinks and mauves. 'What do you think of this?'

'Do you think Dilys would like it?'

'She will if she thinks you chose it all by yourself,' Maudie told him firmly. 'Now, I must get on with my own shopping. Good day to you, Mr Pugh!'

'Just a minute, before you go.'

She turned back. Now what did the

wretched man want?

'I was just wondering what a bodkin was. I don't think I've heard the term before.'

'Oh, it's a gadget for threading elastic through, er, hems,' she explained. She didn't think he could cope with hearing the word 'knickers' spoken aloud.

★   ★   ★

After that uphill battle Maudie headed for the lift. There was a cafeteria on the top floor and she could do with a good strong cup of tea before carrying on with her shopping. With any luck she could find an éclair to go with it, oozing with cream and slathered in chocolate icing. Her mouth watered at the thought.

The nasty little demon on her shoulder reminded her of her plan to lose a few pounds before her wedding day. She ignored it. With all the cycling she did around the parish, one cream cake was surely neither here nor there.

Taking tea at Bentham's always presented a dilemma when you were on your own. Did you try to bag a table first, leaving one of your parcels on the chair to establish ownership, or did you line up for your tea and then have to dither about with your hands full and nowhere to go? Before the war courteous waitresses in black frocks and lace caps had served Bentham's customers, but now there was only the grandmotherly women seated behind the till, and you had to pick up a tray and serve yourself.

The lift arrived but by the time several people had squeezed in there was no room for Maudie. She decided to take the stairs instead, on the grounds that the exercise would undo the damage caused by that chocolate éclair she was looking forward to.

She was halfway up the first flight when she stopped for a moment to survey the department she had just left. She was curious to know if Raymond Pugh had purchased the gift she'd recommended or whether he'd put it down on the counter, deciding to buy a carpet sweeper or something instead. Out of the corner of her eye she saw a familiar figure striding in the direction of the housewares department. It was Miss Mallory's handyman, the mysterious Wilfred. She was still suspicious of the boy's motives, and she hated to think of the doctor's sister being taken in by someone with an eye to the main chance.

She flew back down the stairs, almost knocking over a stout matron carrying a suitcase in either hand. 'Watch where you're going, will you!' the woman bawled.

'Store detective!' Maudie panted. 'Shop-lifters!'

On hearing this declaration the mass of shoppers melted away in front of her, like the Red Sea parting before Moses. She could only hope that the real floorwalker wasn't anywhere nearby, or she might find herself under suspicion. It would not do her career much good if the next edition of the *Midvale Chronicle* carried the headline 'Local Midwife Arrested in Department Store'.

She was in luck. When she entered the housewares department she spotted Wil-fred standing at the checkout counter, paying for what looked like a rather cheap-looking aluminium skillet.

'Are you getting that for Miss Mallory?' she asked. 'For if you are, I don't think she'll care for the quality. She'd be much better off with a good old-fashioned cast-iron frying pan.'

21

The young man's eyes flashed. 'I know what I'm doing, thank you!' he muttered. 'She's already got an iron one, but her arthritis is playing her up and she says her wrists hurt when she lifts anything heavy. She specifically told me to buy something lightweight.'

'I see.'

'No, I don't think you do, lady. I saw you at the house last week, and Miss Mallory had the police round after, asking a lot of questions. I've done nothing wrong and I want to know why you're hounding me like this. Who are you, anyway? Some sort of police spy?'

'I'm a midwife, Wilfred. I worked under Dr Mallory for some years, which is why I went to his funeral — to pay my last respects.'

'I know. I saw you there.' He stared at her with disdain. 'You were wearing some sort of awful uniform.'

'Look here, sir — do you want that frying pan or not?' the sales assistant demanded. 'I haven't got all day, and there's people waiting!'

Embarrassed, Maudie realised that a queue had formed behind them. Far from being annoyed by having to wait, the shoppers were listening avidly to the drama unfolding in front of them.

'Oh, do pay for the wretched thing!' she snapped, standing aside. 'We'll continue this in a minute.' She flashed her teeth at the waiting customers.

When Wilfred had completed his purchase and was clutching the distinctive Bentham's carrier bag to his chest, Maudie returned to the attack.

'I was just going upstairs to have a cup of tea,' she told him. 'Would you care to join me?'

'I suppose so,' he muttered, 'but I'd rather coffee.'

'Coffee, then. Come along, Wilfred.'

It was evidently one of those days. She had been unable to find the tea-towels she'd come to buy, and now there were no éclairs.

'Delivery expected this afternoon,' the motherly woman on the till explained. 'There's Napoleons, though, if you'd care for one of those.'

Maudie regarded the shocking pink icing on the pastries and shook her head. A raisin scone would have to do. Better for her figure, anyway.

Wilfred loaded his plate with two rounds of egg sandwiches and a currant bun. 'I'll go and grab us a table,' he said, leaving her to pay. She sighed, filling her cup from the steaming urn.

'I s'pose you think I'm out to rob the poor old duck,' he said, speaking through a mouthful of half-masticated bread. 'Well I'm not, see! She's getting on a bit and she wants somebody to do a few odd jobs around the place, and I don't charge more than she can afford to pay.'

'Your employment arrangements are none of my business, Wilfred, but you must admit it was a bit much when you came up to me — a stranger — at the funeral to introduce yourself as Dr Mallory's son. You must have known that would cause alarm when everyone knows the doctor was never married.'

'You don't have to be married to have kids.' He picked up another sandwich, peeled back the top layer of bread, and frowned. 'They don't put much egg in these, do they? Highway robbery, that's what I call it.' Replacing the piece of bread, he pushed the sandwich into his mouth until his cheeks bulged.

'Wilfred, I've been around long enough to know that bereaved people are often the target of con men. They read a death notice in the papers and they move in to see what they can get. I've heard of houses being robbed while their owners were away at the funeral service. Or fraud artists turn up claiming to be long-lost relatives, hoping to get a share of the deceased person's goods. It's a wicked world we live in, my boy. Poor Miss Mallory is all alone now. I'd hate to see her taken for a ride.'

'I'm not a con man, Nurse. Yeah, I read about the doc in the newspaper and I came to the funeral, like you said, to pay my respects. And I have come in for some money, but not because I want to rob the old lady! Doc Mallory left me something in his will, and I want to stick around until they pay out. The solicitor chap says it'll take a while before the will is pro-something.'

'Probated,' Maudie said, although she, too, was vague about how these things worked.

'So I think you'd better come back with me and talk to the doc's sister again. She knows my story and I'll let her explain it to you. Me, I'm sick of talking about it. First I had to square it with the lawyers, then the police, and now you. For two pins I'd take off and forget about the money.'

I very much doubt that, young man, Maudie thought, but there was no point in upsetting him further. For all she knew he was spinning her a yarn, and he might do her a mischief while they were walking down that lonely road towards Miss Mallory's cottage.

'Well now, let's do it this way,' she told him. 'I'll stay here and finish my shopping, and you can go back and let Miss Mallory know that I'm coming. Give her a bit of advance warning so she can tidy her hair, that sort of thing. That's what elderly ladies prefer, you know. I'll follow on in a little while. All right?'

'You're on, Nurse.'

And I'll splurge on a taxi, she decided. Just in case the boy was lurking behind a convenient clump of trees with murderous intent, waiting to pounce. Previous experience with deranged men had taught her to be careful. She was no Jemima Puddleduck to be lured into a trap by a Foxy Gentleman.

★　★　★

There was no sign of Wilfred when Maudie arrived at Miss Mallory's cottage in due course. Adding a modest tip to the amount shown on the meter, she paid the cabbie and approached the cottage door. It opened before she could reach for the knocker and she was relieved to find Miss Mallory standing there, with a wintry smile on her wrinkled face.

'I've been expecting you, Nurse. Do come in.'

'Thank you.'

As before, Maudie was invited to sit at the kitchen table, and her hostess joined her, settling into an old-fashioned rocking chair equipped with a squashed satin cushion. A wooden cuckoo burst out of the clock on the wall, announcing the hour.

'I must apologise for having been a bit short with you before,' Miss Mallory began.

'Not at all. Losing your only brother must have been difficult for you.'

'Yes, indeed, but it wasn't just that. I'm afraid I resented the fact that you seemed — how shall I put it? Over-interested in my private business.'

Maudie felt her cheeks growing hot. 'I'm so sorry if I gave offence. It's just that as a nurse I'm used to taking charge, I suppose.'

'Having thought about it, I realise that you had my best interests at heart.'

'One does hear such awful things about bereaved people being taken advantage of while they are in a vulnerable state.'

'Quite so, but in this case there really is nothing amiss.'

'Oh, but that young man definitely told me that he is Dr Mallory's son! And as you have explained that your brother was never married you can see why my suspicions were aroused.'

'And you won't rest until you get to the bottom of this, will you, Nurse?'

Maudie blushed again, and waited.

'I suppose nothing will satisfy you until you get a full explanation! Well, poor little Wilfred has given me permission to speak, so I suppose I must. It's rather a long story, so would you care for a cup of tea before I begin?'

'No, thank you, Miss Mallory; I had my elevenses at Bentham's. But do have one yourself if you wish. I shan't mind waiting.'

'I'm not thirsty, either. So shall we get on with it? Wilfred has gone to the library for me, so we shan't be interrupted.'

22

'As you may have guessed, I am many years younger than my brother, Nurse Rouse. He was born when my parents had been married less than two years, while I came along when he was almost grown up. Mother told me later that I was what people used to call a change-of-life baby. I expect you know all about that, Nurse.'

Maudie did. For some reason the hormonal changes that took place as women approached the menopause sometimes caused a new burst of fertility, as a result of which she could find herself pregnant in her forties, just when she expected that the experience of giving birth and new motherhood was all behind her.

'I tell you this to explain why I didn't really get to know my brother until I moved here to Midvale after the war. By the time I'd started primary school he was already studying to become a doctor, and he never returned to our home again, except for the occasional short visit. By the time I was grown up myself, we had gone our separate ways.'

'I believe you said that you were a missionary in India?'

'Yes, and no. I trained as a teacher and I did spend several years serving in the mission field, but it was in that capacity. Other than teaching hymns and telling Bible stories I didn't actually take part in the work of converting the natives. I left that to the Reverend Mr and Mrs Potts, who were my superiors there. I did hope that my brother would get the call to follow me to the mission field. Doctors were badly needed there. But he insisted that doctors were needed in England, too, and this was where he belonged. When he retired in 1927 he went down to Devon, with the idea that when I returned to England I should join him there, to keep house for him. And that was when he first met Wilfred.'

'He met Wilfred? But how old was the boy then?'

'Just a few hours old. You see, Evan didn't take kindly to retirement, so he agreed to serve as a locum, filling in for local doctors who needed a holiday, or who perhaps wanted to attend lectures dealing with some new discovery in medicine. Evan was always interested in new developments. Why, I remember how excited he was back in 1921 when those Canadian doctors discovered insulin. Before that a diagnosis of diabetes meant a certain death sentence, but of course you must know all about that.'

'You were telling me about Wilfred,' Maudie reminded her, trying to curb her impatience.

'Oh, yes. Now where was I? Yes. My brother was filling in for one doctor when he had a call from an orphanage that was run by an order of nuns. A very young baby boy had been left on their doorstep, wrapped in a towel, and they wanted the doctor to look him over to make sure he was all right. Evan duly called on them and pronounced the baby to be in good health.'

'And that baby was Wilfred?'

'Yes, although he wasn't called that then. The nuns liked to name their foundlings after saints, so this time they chose an English saint, Wilfrid of Northumbria, changing the spelling slightly to give the boy a more up-to-date name. To help him fit in when he went to school, I suppose.'

'But I'm guessing the story didn't end there?'

'Oh, no. I had a letter from Evan saying that the nuns had asked him to stand godfather to the baby, and he had agreed to do so.'

So Mr Blunt was right after all, Maudie thought. 'And did Dr Mallory continue to keep an eye on the boy after that?'

'Yes, he did. Perhaps you're not aware of this, Nurse, but when my brother was young there was a great deal more to being a godparent than sending gifts for birthdays and Christmas. It meant keeping an eye on the child's moral and spiritual development as well. In fact, there was a time when godparents were expected to bring up the child in the event of its parents' death.'

Maudie gasped. 'Are you saying that Dr Mallory adopted Wilfred?'

'Not in so many words. He couldn't do that, you see, being unmarried. He did do things with the boy, though. Took him fishing, or to football matches, that sort of thing.'

'And in the meantime Wilfred stayed on at the orphanage?'

Miss Mallory sighed. 'That was the sad thing. The nuns did their best to get the children adopted into good families, but somehow they had no success with Wilfred. Evan always felt badly about that, I know. They made several attempts to foster him out, with a view to eventual adoption if things worked well, but something always seemed to go wrong. I've talked to the boy about it since he came here and I've learned quite a bit about his background.

'He went to one family where there was already an older boy and a little girl, but he was bullied by the boy, who called him names for being an orphan, and the little girl followed suit. Wilfred fought back and in the end there was so much discord in the home that the parents couldn't cope. He was sent back to the orphanage.'

'How sad,' Maudie murmured.

'The nuns did try again, I understand, but each time the adoption fell through. He went to a childless couple who changed their minds when they learned that the wife was expecting her own child after ten years of marriage. Then he went to a place where he was accused of stealing the money that had been left out with the milk bottles to pay the milkman. Poor Wilfred hadn't done it, but he couldn't prove his innocence, so it was back to the orphanage.' Miss Mallory leaned forward, putting her head in her hands. 'I think if you don't mind, Nurse, I'll have that cup of tea after all. I find all this quite distressing.'

'Let me make it,' Maudie said, getting up.

'No, no, I wouldn't dream of it. I'll be right in no time. Will you join me after all?'

'Yes, please.'

Sitting quietly while Miss Mallory bustled about, Maudie thought over what she had just heard. It was an old story. Jane Eyre, the heroine of Charlotte Brontë's book, had been falsely accused by cousins and subsequently sent off to a strict boarding school. Maudie had no doubt that such things had happened years ago. They were probably still happening, for there were a great many war orphans in Britain today who must have tragic stories to tell. But as for Wilfred Fletcher, who knew whether his tales were real or invented?

'Did Dr Mallory keep in touch with Wilfred right up until his death?' Maudie asked, when she had accepted a cup of Earl Grey tea and a digestive biscuit. She thoroughly disliked Earl Grey but it was hot and wet, and she was prepared to suffer in a good cause.

'No, unfortunately. He lost touch with the boy when war broke out and he was called back into service on the home front. He came to Midvale in 1940.'

'So you didn't know the boy at that stage either.'

'I met him for the first time at Evan's funeral. He came up to me to introduce himself, saying that he'd read about it in the newspapers and had come to pay his respects.'

So that part of Wilfred's story was at least true, Maudie thought. 'It must have been quite a shock if he claimed to be your nephew,' she suggested.

Miss Mallory laughed. 'He said nothing of the sort to me, Nurse. He didn't dare, I suppose.'

'Well, he certainly told me that he was the doctor's son.'

'Silly boy! I suppose in a way Evan was the nearest thing to a real father he ever had. I expected him to turn up some day, though. After Evan retired for the second time he came here to live with me, as you know, and he told me he'd been thinking about the boy a lot.

' 'I'm going to leave him something in my will,' he told me. 'The boy needs a leg-up to get him started in the world.' I didn't mind about that. Evan had already helped me to buy this little house when I returned from India. I had my savings, but I could never have managed that on my own. Evan did quite well out of selling the practice to those young doctors, and he could afford to support the two of us with something left over for the boy.'

'Does this mean you'll be taking Wilfred in to live under your roof?' Maudie asked, hoping she wouldn't get her head bitten off for asking.

'No, Nurse, it does not! When the time comes he'll take his money and go. My solicitor will see to that. If I needed to take in a lodger it would be a lady of my own age and background, not a gangling youth.'

So Maudie made her excuses and went on her way, pleased to have solved the mystery but not quite satisfied as to the probable outcome. Would Wilfred be satisfied with the money left to him by his mentor, or would he hang around, hoping for something more?

Perhaps the lad was all that the kindly Miss Mallory believed him to be, or perhaps he was not. It wouldn't hurt for the police to keep a file of that young man, just in case. She made up her mind to mention it to Dick when next she saw him.

A little cloud of gloom seemed to have settled over her head, like one of those bubbles in a comic book strip that lets you in on the character's state of mind. Dick would soon be off to the police college at Hendon, and once again she would be lost without his cheerful company.

23

Maudie was kept busy with work for the next few days. Three women were expecting babies in the near future and she kept a careful check on them. It was bad luck that they each lived at the furthest points of her territory; she wished she could collect them all together in one place, which would save her legs. She only hoped they wouldn't all go into labour at once. If the worst happened she would have to call in one of the doctors to assist.

One woman, Marie Jukes, was an old hand at motherhood. She was now expecting her fifth and Maudie anticipated that her labour, once begun, would proceed fairly swiftly. It never did to take anything for granted, though. Complications could arise with any patient.

Another mother-to-be, Pamela Stokes, needed a great deal of reassurance. 'I want this baby so much, Nurse,' she told

Maudie, 'but I'm really scared of what I have to go through to get it. Labour is terrible, isn't it? I read in a magazine that it's ten times as bad as the worst toothache. I've had toothache and I know I couldn't stand anything worse.'

Maudie wished that people wouldn't write such rot. Childbirth was no joke and every mother had to go through it, but first-timers didn't know what to expect and so their imaginations ran riot.

'Try not to worry too much, Pamela,' she soothed. 'I promise you you'll be quite safe with me.'

'My great aunt died in childbirth,' Pamela moaned. 'What if it happens to me, Nurse?'

'Your great aunt? I expect that was quite a few years ago, wasn't it? Things are different today. Now then, is everything ready for Baby? Have you prepared a cot for him or her?'

The third mother, Betty Cram, was quite philosophical about the whole process, having been through it once before. 'I'll be thankful when this is over and the baby is here,' she said. 'I'm so sick of wearing this ghastly maternity dress, and I'm looking forward to the day when I can see my feet again. Is everything all right, Nurse? I wasn't this fat with our Timmy.'

'All is well, Mrs Cram. You've been putting on about five pounds a month, which is just right. Your blood pressure is fine and your ankles aren't swollen. Now you have my telephone number, don't you? Get your hubby to call me when labour starts and before you know it Timmy will have a little brother or sister.'

'I want a girl this time, Nurse.'

Maudie laughed. 'I'm afraid I can't promise you that, Mrs Cram! And once the baby is here you'll love it no matter what sex it turns out to be.'

'Of course I will. Just so long as it's got all its fingers and toes.'

'And there's absolutely no reason why it shouldn't be a healthy child. Is Timmy looking forward to becoming a big brother?'

Mrs Cram wrinkled her nose. 'He says he'd rather have a puppy! I hope he isn't going to be jealous. He's had our undivided attention for seven years. This may come as a shock to him, especially when the new one keeps us all awake at night.'

'You'll have to ask your hubby to give him a bit of extra attention, then. And if family and friends bring gifts for the new baby, I suggest you have something on hand to keep Timmy occupied. Tell him it's a present from the baby.'

'That's a good idea, Nurse. He's been wanting a signal for his train set but his birthday is a long way off and we haven't done anything about it. I'll get Jack to pop into the toyshop in Midvale and see what they've got. I wouldn't be surprised if he comes back with more than one thing. He loves that train set as much as Timmy does, on account of he never had one as a boy. Jack comes from a big family and there was never the money to spare for fancy toys like that. I think he's in his second childhood now.'

'Ah, well, better he plays with trains than goes chasing after other women!' Maudie said, laughing.

★ ★ ★

Maudie spent two days a week helping out at the surgery. Dr Ransome seemed pleasant and competent, and she could tell that the patients seemed to like him.

'He's easier to get on with than that Dr Dean over at Midvale,' she heard one old man say to another. 'Dean asked me all sorts of questions about things I never had wrong with me, and when I said as I'd come about my piles he says he doesn't want to listen to my whole life history. I come away with nothing for me piles. I'd have done better to talk to Nurse Rouse!'

'I hope you told the chap where to get off, the useless article!' his friend said.

'Nah. I couldn't be bothered. Mind you, it's all free now with this newfangled Health Service, but if I'd had to go there and pay like we used to, I'd have given him a piece of my mind!'

Maudie noticed that Dr Ransome still didn't have his professional certificates up on the wall, and when they were having their mid-morning cup of tea she mentioned this again. 'The patients really do take an interest in these things, you know.'

'I'll get around to it some day,' he told her. 'My flat is in absolute chaos. All my stuff is in boxes and I haven't got unpacked yet. Goodness knows when I'll ever get straight. I think I need a good woman to sort me out! In the meantime, would you like to hang up your nursing diplomas here, Nurse? The wall won't look as bare then.'

'Oh, that's all right, Doctor. I have them on the wall of my office in the parish hall.' She made a mental note to take them down in case he dropped into the office one day and saw them there. She might leave the midwifery one hanging there but not the one from her nursing school. So far she had managed to avoid telling him where she had done her training, because if he knew it was at Mary and Martha's he'd realise that she was on to him.

She longed to tell someone about her suspicions that this Dr Julian Ransome was a fake, but who could she tell? The only people she really cared to confide in were Dick Bryant and Joan Blunt, but as yet she wasn't prepared to speak to either one. As a policeman, Dick would feel honour-bound to start an investigation into Dr Ransome's credentials, which would be unfair if the man had done nothing wrong. And as a vicar's wife Joan Blunt knew how to keep confidences to herself, but she'd think Maudie was stark, staring mad. After all, the evidence was pretty thin. He was a former left-hander using his right hand now, was he? Perhaps he had trained himself to make the switch, although Maudie couldn't imagine why he should want to.

Her mind went back to her school days. She must have been in Standard One at the time, or was it Standard Two? Anyway, a new boy had joined the class — Robert, his name was — and he was left-handed. Maudie vividly recalled the horror she felt when the teacher tied the child's left hand behind his back and forced him to use the right to form the letters on his slate. By the time the summer holidays came Robert had developed a facial tic and had started to stammer.

Maudie had never fathomed why there was this prejudice against the use of the left hand, not in the twentieth century. Perhaps in the olden days it was thought to have had something to do with witchcraft. Surely Julian Ransome hadn't suffered under such nonsense? He had certainly never mentioned anything like that back in the heady days of new love, when they had talked about the minutiae of their lives.

More significant was the apparent change in Julian Ransome's personality. What had become of the arrogant, impatient man she had known? Had he really mellowed to such an extent? Of course it was thirteen years since he'd graduated as a doctor, and since then he'd been the through a war. That must have wrought some changes.

Still, the idea of discussing any of this with her friends seemed impossible. She was making mountains out of molehills and she'd better pull herself together before the men in white coats came to fetch her!

And then a letter landed on her doormat that changed everything.

24

Maudie's heart seemed to beat a little faster when she picked up the letter with the hospital crest on the back flap of the envelope. Ripping it open with her thumb, she pulled out the neatly written sheets of paper, checking the signature first. Yes, this was what she'd been waiting for — news from her old classmate, Sister Doris Martin, nee Perry.

I must apologise for not having written sooner, the letter began. *It's been like Paddy's market here on the ward and I haven't got off on time for what seems like ages.*

Maudie skipped over the accounts of what was happening in Male Surgical, meaning to return to all that later. Under normal circumstances she would have read these with interest, but she had more important things on her mind.

Then it took me a while to pluck up the courage to delve into Bob's letters again.

It's been hard for me since Bob was killed and last year I almost destroyed the lot, thinking I had to let go of the past, but something held me back. Now I'm glad I didn't! I found the letter I was looking for, in which he mentioned Julian Ransome's death. I trust you won't mind if I don't send the original; most of it is a bit personal. I've copied out the reference you want, and I hope that will do. You'll never guess what happened here on Thursday! Matron . . .

'Never mind Matron!' Maudie muttered, hunting for the next sheet. Why couldn't Doris have numbered the pages? 'Ah, here we go!'

'*Sorry to say that your Julian Ransome's been killed. The lorry he was driving hit a land mine and he was blown to smithereens. I don't know what became of that medical orderly I told you about. I didn't see it happen myself. I thought you'd like to know about this, as you knew each other at Mary and Martha's, but don't please don't let this news add to your worries about me. Either my number will come up or it* won't, so *there's no point in thinking morbid thoughts.'*

Maudie sighed. Poor Bob's time had indeed come, and now she was forcing poor Doris to face that yet again. How long did it take for people to get over losing loved ones in a time of war? Did they ever truly recover?

She sat down with the letter still clutched in her hand. So here was proof that Julian Ransome had been killed while serving in North Africa. Or was it? Bob Martin hadn't actually seen it happen; he had only heard about it. And who was the medical orderly he'd referred to? And why had he told his wife about him, unless the chap was another Mary and Martha's person?

Maudie doubted that it was significant in any way, but she would write back to Doris, asking her what Bob had told her about the orderly. Meanwhile, she needed to verify Julian's death. In wartime there must be cases of mistaken identity or other muddles. In fact, there had been one involving a soldier from Midvale. His family there had received word of his death and the *Midvale Chronicle* had interviewed the parents and written an article based on the young man's life. There hadn't been much to say, really. John Jones had attended school locally and then had become an apprentice in the building trade. He had joined up at the age of eighteen and had been killed at Dieppe.

The real story appeared quite some time later. The bereaved mother had been busily running sheets through the mangle when her son walked into the scullery with a cheerful, 'Hello, Mum!'

'It was a wonder I didn't get my arm stuck in the rollers,' she was quoted as saying later. 'I thought for a minute he was a ghost, come to say goodbye to his poor old mum.'

Maudie had thought at the time that with all the upheaval of war it was a miracle that there weren't many more such mistakes of that sort. And there must have been dozens — no, hundreds — of chaps called Smith or Jones in the services. The army could easily have muddled them up, even if they did all have numbers allotted to them, as if they were cars or something.

She dragged her mind back to the present. She must write to the War Office, asking for more details. Could they make a search on Julian's name alone? She had no idea what his number would have been; in fact, she didn't know which regiment he'd served with.

Of course she knew about the Royal Army Medical Corps, whose members provided medical services to military personnel and their families in times of both war and peace. In fact, after her sad let-down by Julian Ransome, she had attempted to join Queen Alexandra's Royal Nursing Corps, which came under the umbrella of the RAMC. She'd been sent away with a flea in her ear and told to take up a civilian post where her midwifery skills would be put to good use.

But in order to find out more, would she have to provide details of where and when Julian had been serving when he was killed? Was he attached to Bob's regiment in particular, or just a member-at-large of the RAMC, sent here and there as the need arose? She had absolutely no idea how these things worked.

Right, then — she would put off writing to either the War Office or the RAMC until she had learned more from Doris. Question one: what was Bob's regiment? Two: what did Doris know about the doctors who had served there? Lastly: what had Bob meant by that reference to Julian and a medical orderly?

It was probably nothing, of course. They could have been taking part in an improvised game of cricket or football, and the two men had helped their side to win, with a stroke of brilliant play. Or perhaps the orderly had committed some misdemeanour and Julian had put him on a charge. There could even have been a court martial, nothing at all to do with Maudie's present quest. Still, she must leave no stone unturned.

Thinking again about the young soldier, John Jones, she wondered what had become of him. Had he survived the war and returned to Midvale after being demobbed? How thankful his poor mother must have been to see him safely home again. War was hell, and it wasn't just those in the armed forces who suffered. Their loved ones on the home front had to endure the agony that went with fearing for their safety.

Well, now! If Julian had been killed, his parents at Godalming would have been notified. Or, if it had been a mistake, they would know where he was at present. They would be pretty elderly if they were still alive. The sister, Veronica, would still be around though, but if she had married and changed her name she might be harder to find.

There must be ways in which these people could be tracked down. Perhaps there were voters' lists? Street directories? Maudie could enquire at the library about the possibilities.

A rattling sound came from the pantry and her heart seemed to miss a beat. She had left the window open to rid the place of the smell of curried rice and had forgotten to close it again. A large burglar was hardly likely to squeeze through, but a child or a teenager might. She picked up her umbrella and tiptoed through.

Perkin, the vicarage cat, lifted his head in disdain. He had just polished off the remains of half a pound of butter and was licking his lips in satisfaction.

'You wretched cat!' she roared. 'You wouldn't come home with me when I offered you a place to stay, oh, no! But you feel it's all right to pop in for a free meal, I suppose!'

'Yerrup!' the cat moaned, and promptly regurgitated the stolen goods onto Maudie's spotless marble shelf.

'You fiend!' she yelled, and the cat leapt onto the windowsill and was gone. Muttering, she went to fetch hot water and disinfectant.

25

Maudie stayed clasped in Dick's arms, with her head buried in his shoulder. They were curled up on the sagging sofa in her cottage, oblivious to the spring rainstorm outside.

'I've missed you,' she whispered.

'I've missed you too, old girl, but at least those wretched exams are over.'

'How do you think you did?'

'Hard to tell. I think I did not badly on the essay questions but I was a bit flummoxed by the multiple-choice section. They give you four statements on a certain subject and you have to pick the one that you hope is the right answer. The only trouble is, they fix it so that two statements sound possible.'

'Oh, well, they don't expect you to get a hundred per cent in order to pass, do they?'

'No, but I wanted to do better than just scrape through. Even if I pass I'll have to wait for a vacancy to be promoted to sergeant and I don't want to be pipped at the post by someone with a higher mark.'

Maudie smiled at him. 'Has all that studying given you a taste for the legal side of things? Perhaps you'd like to be a solicitor or a barrister now?'

This made him chuckle. 'I don't think I can aspire to that. If they ever start letting people with no university degrees start practising law, I'd rather be a judge.'

'A hanging judge?' Maudie asked, entering into the spirit of things.

'That's right. I can just see myself putting on the black cap and saying, 'You will be taken from here to a place of execution to be hanged by the neck until you are dead. And may the Lord have mercy on your soul!''

Maudie wasn't sure if this bit of gallows humour reflected Dick's true feelings, and she wasn't about to press the point. She shuddered. 'I don't think I could do it myself.'

'That's because you're a midwife. Your job is all about life. Anyway, let's forget about my exams for now. Pass or fail, I've done my best and now we'll have to wait and see what happens.'

Maudie kissed him again. 'I wish you didn't have to leave tomorrow,' she muttered when she had recovered her breath.

'It won't be for long, and I'll be able to pop back up on the motorbike now and then.'

'I know, but we haven't seen much of each other lately.'

He held her away from him and looked into her eyes. 'I'm doing this for us, Maudie. You know that, don't you? Even so, if you really don't want this, it's not too late for me to back out. I mean it, Maudie. I love you and I'd do anything to make you happy.'

'Of course you must go!' she assured him. 'And you can't chop and change at the last moment, or the powers that be might mark you down as unreliable. That could affect your sergeant's posting, too. Don't worry about me. I'll find plenty to do to keep me busy until you get back.'

'Well, then, you can get busy with our wedding plans! I'm not having it put off again, Maudie Rouse.'

She smiled. 'I'll go and see Mr Blunt tomorrow and give him a choice of dates in July. I've been putting it off because of his accident, but he's on the mend now.'

'And what about the honeymoon? We'll have to think about booking well ahead of time if we hope to get into a guesthouse or hotel, particularly if we choose to go to a popular resort. Now that the war is well and truly over people are beginning to take holidays again, and July is the peak period when the kiddies are being let out of school.'

'I've been thinking about that. I hate the idea of arriving at some hotel shedding confetti all over the place and having people giving us arch looks.'

'I can't say I'd fancy that myself,' Dick agreed.

'And neither do I want to travel in a crowded train to somewhere far-flung, especially if it's full of harassed parents and unruly children, and we might have to stand in the corridor all the way. I had quite enough of that during the war. We don't know how much time off you'll get, and if it's only a weekend that does limit us a bit.'

'So what are you saying? You can't mean you don't want a honeymoon at all?'

'I'm saying we should spend our honeymoon here, in this cottage. Just think about it for a minute, Dick! We'd have all the comforts of home. No exhausting travel, and it wouldn't cost us a penny.'

Dick studied his nails. 'It sounds all right, but would it work? What would you do if you were called to a confinement? I know you, Maudie Rouse! You'd have to go to the perishing woman, and where would that leave me? Oh, I know that sounds selfish, but I'm only going to get married once and I do want everything to be perfect for us.'

'I've thought about that. We'll tell a white lie and say we're going to — oh, I don't know ... Blackpool maybe, or Stratford-upon-Avon to see Shakespeare's birthplace? People can wave us off and we'll go to the station to catch the appropriate train, only we'll double back and creep in the back door here.'

'It sounds promising,' Dick admitted.

'There's only one problem. At that time of year it's still daylight until ten o'clock at night. How do we get back here without being spotted? We'd have to pass the shop and Mrs Hatch would be bound to notice us.'

'I think you can leave that part of it to me,' Dick said. 'Perhaps I can get my mates to create a diversion. I'd have to let them in on the secret, of course, but none of them are Llandyfan chaps so I don't think the truth will leak out. Good grief! Have you seen the time? I'd better get home and catch a few hours' sleep, for I'm off to Hendon in the morning.'

Saying good night took some time, but at last Maudie closed the door behind Dick and stood listening until the sound of his departing motorcycle receded into the distance. Then she made herself a cup of hot milk and took it up to bed.

She had barely got settled when the phone rang. Struggling into her comfortable old dressing gown, she hurried downstairs and snatched the earpiece off the phone.

'Nurse Rouse speaking.'

The calm voice of Jack Cram came across the line. 'Can you come, Nurse? My Betty's started. She says to tell you the pains are coming every five minutes and she's sure it's the real thing.'

'I'll be right there, Mr Cram.'

'Righty-ho! I'd better get back, then. Our Timmy is up and making a thorough nuisance of himself and I'll have to take charge of him. Betty doesn't want him to hear her hollering, but she says she can't hold back much longer.'

'Goodbye, Mr Cram!' Maudie hung up and fled back upstairs to dress. So much for a good night's rest!

★　★　★

Much later, when Maudie finally stumbled into bed, she found herself unable to fall asleep. Mrs Cram was safely delivered of a lovely little boy; not the daughter she been hoping for, yet both parents had expressed their delight in Baby Cram.

'We'll call him John, after his dad,'

Betty had said happily. 'Tim is called after my father and that's fine, but Jack's dad was Ebenezer and I don't think you can saddle a kiddie with that name, can you? Not in this day and age.'

'That might be a bit much when he gets into secondary school and has to write out his full name on the top of every exam paper,' Maudie agreed. It hadn't been too bad for her, having to put Maudie Grace Rouse on her own papers, but she'd sympathised with a friend who'd been landed with the names Gwendolyn Patricia Madeleine Seagrove. All perfectly decent names, of course, but time-consuming when you had to keep writing them out in full on every page.

Now there was an idea! When reporting the birth to Dr Ransome she could introduce the subject of names into the conversation, asking him what his middle name was. Her Julian's second name was Peter. Any little clue that would help her to learn the truth about the sexy, amiable doctor who was now working in their midst might help.

Maudie was beginning to think that she

was trying make bricks without straw as the Bible said, yet the more far-fetched her suspicions seemed, the more she was determined to keep going in her quest for the truth.

26

True to her word, Maudie went to call on the vicar. Joan Blunt greeted her at the kitchen door. 'Hello, Nurse. Come to see Harold, have you?'

'Yes, please. I want to know how he's doing, of course, but I'd like to speak to him about the wedding, please, if he's feeling up to it or not too busy.'

'He'll be glad of the interruption. They told him at the hospital that he's to do very little until he gets the all-clear at his appointment next week, but he's bored to tears. He says there's nothing on the wireless, the papers are full of gloom and doom, and he's played patience until he wants to throw the cards out of the window.'

Maudie laughed. 'He must be getting better!'

'I tend to agree with you, Nurse. It's my poor Perkin I'm worried about this morning. He's off his food and I was about to phone the vet.'

'Oh, I shouldn't worry about that cat,' Maudie told her. 'Let him sleep it off. He'll be right as rain in a day or two.'

'What do you mean? You haven't even examined the poor beast.'

'Oh, but I got a good look at him last night, right after he'd finished demolishing my week's supply of butter! I left the pantry window open by mistake and the temptation must have been too much for him.'

Poor Mrs Blunt looked stricken. 'I don't know how to apologise, Nurse. I shall make it good of course. Just let me get my purse and I'll reimburse you.'

'Never mind about that. It was just as much my fault as Perkin's. I wouldn't have mentioned it except that you were about to have a needless trip to the vet.'

'Well, if you're sure.'

'Of course. Isn't that your phone? I don't mind waiting while you answer it.'

'I'll let Harold deal with it. It will give him something to do. How are things on the work front? Are there any new little parishioners for us?'

'Betty Cram delivered last night. They've got another little boy. They're going to call him John, after his father.'

'How lovely. I'm so glad they've decided to give him a sensible name. So many babies get called after American film stars these days. Clark, or Errol, or Tallulah. I hope they don't get teased when they start school. Children can be so nasty at times. It quite makes one believe in original sin!'

The vicar entered the room looking pleased with himself. Maudie stared at him in puzzlement. He looked different somehow. Then it struck her: he wasn't wearing his clerical collar. And why should he be? It wouldn't match the blue-striped pyjamas and the Jaeger dressing gown he had on!

'Did I hear you discussing baptismal names?' he enquired.

'Nurse was just telling me that the Crams have their new baby. They are calling him John.'

'Very suitable. When I was newly ordained I was asked to baptize a child with the name Amiens. A little girl it was, too. The father had served in the Great War, but don't ask me why he wanted to remember it in that way. I refused, of course.'

'Oh, dear,' Maudie said. 'What did he say to that?'

'Nothing I care to repeat now, Nurse. I believe he went off and joined the Nonconformists.'

'Who was that on the telephone, dear?' Mrs Blunt asked. 'Are we expecting company? Because Nurse is here to speak to you about her wedding.'

'That detective inspector from Midvale wants to call round. He says he has some news for me about the anonymous letters I've been getting, so I must just dash up and change. I can't greet him looking like this.'

Maudie's eyes opened wide. 'Well, that's a turn-up for the books!' she whispered, when the vicar had gone.

Her friend looked at her in amusement. 'And I suppose you'd like to be in at the kill! Why not stay and hear what the inspector has to say? I'm sure Harold won't mind. After all, if it hadn't been for you, anything could have happened. He might have died there on the road, or been run over by something else that came speeding along. I know how grateful he is.'

The inspector arrived in due course, with a younger sidekick in tow. He looked meaningfully at Maudie, who chose not to take the hint.

'I should like Nurse to stay,' Mrs Blunt said. 'Just in case your news might affect my husband badly. He still hasn't fully recovered from his accident and his doctors say he must go carefully for the moment.'

Maudie didn't think that the vicar was in imminent danger of needing artificial respiration but she nodded importantly, fingering the watch she wore pinned to the bosom of her uniform dress. Mrs Blunt shepherded them into the drawing room where they all sat down with the exception of the constable, who stood stolidly behind the inspector's chair.

'The Met have apprehended a suspect by the name of William Marsh,' the inspector began. 'He admits to having sent threatening letters to you, Mr Blunt.'

'William Marsh? I don't think we know anyone by that name, do we, dear?' The vicar looked at his wife, who shook her head.

'Be that as it may, he has confessed to it, and he is certainly aware of your address here in Llandyfan. A search of his flat turned up a list of addresses and samples of stationery that matches the letter you turned over to us.'

'Lists, you say? Did he target other people as well? But why pick on me, Inspector? How did this man obtain my address, and what was his purpose in writing to me? Is he deranged, perhaps?'

'By his own admission this is one of those sad stories coming out of the war, sir. Apparently his son, an only child, was a conscientious objector. He went before a tribunal to plead exemption from active service on moral grounds, but was turned down and sent to prison. While he was there he was repeatedly beaten and bullied by other prisoners and eventually he hanged himself. Marsh insists that the boy was murdered by other inmates.'

This was not the first time that Maudie had heard such a story. Other men, who felt it was their duty to fight for king and country, often despised 'conchies', as they were referred to.

* * *

Maudie was torn two ways when she thought about this. She knew that if she were a man she would definitely have joined up to do her bit, yet could she have brought herself to kill an enemy? She wasn't at all sure about that. Perhaps it was because she was a woman, and women are born to nurture others, not to kill. And she could understand that some men with strong religious convictions might be against taking life.

But what if the feared invasion had taken place? Would the objectors have meekly surrendered to Hitler's advancing troops? She had thrilled to Winston Churchill's famous speech — 'We shall fight them in the street' — and would have gone out to do what she could, even if armed only with a rolling pin. She blushed now to recall her naivety.

'Marsh has been hounding all the people who served on that tribunal which, as he sees it, were the indirect cause of his boy's death. One of those concerned is a prominent Member of Parliament today, and the Met have had his home under surveillance since this thing started. Marsh was apprehended as he was pushing the latest round of letters through the letterbox.'

'But I still don't understand,' the vicar said. 'I was never on any tribunal. Why would this chap think I was?'

'Now that I don't know, Mr Blunt. This whole thing is still under investigation. We just wanted to let you know that you're no longer in any danger. Mind you, I'd be prepared to bet that by the sound of it this chap never intended to carry out his threats. A psychiatrist who has interviewed Marsh suggests that he just wanted to lash out at someone. His wife died last year and perhaps the added grief has finally tipped him over the edge.'

'Perhaps that's why he's picked on me,

then, as a man of the cloth. He may feel that God has let him down, you know.'

'Perhaps he does,' Maudie pointed out. 'But why you? There must be thousands of clergymen in England to choose from.'

'As I said, Mr Blunt, the investigation is ongoing. You'll be informed of progress as soon as there is anything to report. Meanwhile, you can sleep safely in your bed without having to worry any more about this nasty business.'

'Thank you for coming, Inspector,' Mrs Blunt said. 'I'll show you out.'

'I don't know about being safe in my bed, Nurse,' the vicar said in a low voice, 'but I do think I'm going to have to go right there now, and lie down. I feel quite washed out. And as for not worrying any more, I don't see how he can make that out. It's true there is no connection between the letter writer and my accident, but how can I rest until I know why this poor chap is after me?'

'That's right, up you come,' Maudie said, hooking her left arm under his left one in the approved fashion, helping him to his feet. 'I'll just see you into bed and test your temperature, pulse and respiration, and then you can have a nice nap.'

'Oh, but you came to discuss your wedding, didn't you, Nurse? I'm so sorry; this business has made it slip my mind.'

'Never mind that now,' Maudie assured him. 'There's nothing that can't wait. Just don't give away all the Saturdays in July in the meantime, all right?'

27

A jagged fork of lightning sent a blinding light into Maudie's living room. A loud crack of thunder followed within seconds, telling her that the storm was right overhead. Wincing, she ran to draw the curtains across the window, jumping back as another flash lit up the evening sky.

Cowering in her armchair, she hoped that the storm would soon pass over before any serious damage was done. She had a feeling that she'd soon be hearing from at least one of her expectant mothers. Although doctors tended to dismiss it as an old wives' tale, midwives knew that a storm often brought a baby along with it, as if it jarred them awake in the womb, telling them to get moving.

Sure enough, the thunderstorm had barely deteriorated into a distant rumble when the telephone rang. She picked up the receiver reluctantly, afraid that lightning might somehow travel along the lines to finish her off.

'Is that the midwife?' The line was crackling and she could just make out the calm voice of what sounded like an older woman.

'Yes, Maudie Rouse speaking. Can I help you?'

'I hope so. Awful storm, isn't it? I'm calling on behalf of my neighbour, Pamela Stokes.'

'Is she in labour?'

'Seems to be. It's the husband I'm worried about, Nurse. He's hopping about like a flea on a blanket, making no end of a fuss. Having a baby is bad enough without all that going on.'

'Don't worry, I'll deal with him. Will you be all right getting home?'

'Oh, yes. It's coming down in buckets but the thunder has stopped. I'll hang up now, then, so you can get started.'

'I'm on my way.'

Maudie sighed. What sort of man would send an elderly neighbour out in the storm to the nearest phone box, when he could have done that for himself? Well, it was his first child, and perhaps he was too frazzled to think straight. She supposed it was praiseworthy of him to be concerned, but she'd need to get rid of him when she got there. She couldn't manage with him dithering at her heels.

Lightning filled the room again. It looked as if this was going to be one of those circular storms where the thunder and lightning kept coming back. Reluctantly, she picked up the phone again to call the taxi. She was not about to cycle the length of the parish in that lot! It wouldn't help mother or baby if she was struck down on the road.

A frantic husband greeted her when she scrambled out of the cab. 'Thank goodness you've come, Nurse. My poor wife! It's terrible, just terrible!'

'Can you pay the driver for me, Mr Stokes?' Maudie had no intention of charging the taxi to him, but this would keep him busy for a few minutes while she assessed the situation. Sadly, he was back at her side in no time.

'I gave the chap five bob and told him to keep the change. It's not right to leave

Pammie alone. She's in pain, Nurse. Why is she having pain?'

'Just take me to Mrs Stokes and we'll discuss that in a minute.'

Maudie followed him up the lino-covered stairs, taking note of the truly awful wallpaper on the way up. Dark green leaves rioted over blood-red trellises, their tendrils reaching out as if to snatch at the unwary passerby.

I'd have pain too, if I had to look at that lot every day, she decided, but there was no time to ponder the dreadful taste of the person who had executed the design.

'You're coming along very nicely, Mrs Stokes,' Maudie told her patient when she had examined her. Pamela was a long way from being fully dilated so it could be quite some time before the baby was born.

'Can you make it stop, Nurse? I've changed my mind! I don't want to do this!'

Maudie smiled kindly. 'I'm afraid it's nine months too late for that, my dear.'

'Ow! Here comes another one! Oh, I

could kill that Derek Stokes! If I live through this I'll never let him near me again!'

'That's right, dear,' Maudie said, grinning as she fastened the blood pressure cuff around her patient's arm. She had heard it all before.

Derek Stokes had been loitering outside the door during Maudie's examination of his wife. He burst in now, red-faced and truculent. 'Something's wrong, isn't it? Poor Pammie! I heard her cry out. Are you sure you know what you're doing? She should be in hospital! Shall I call an ambulance?'

Maudie patted his shoulder in what she hoped was a reassuring manner. 'You can take it from me that your wife is quite all right, Mr Stokes. Everything is coming along as it should. There is absolutely no need for her to go to hospital.'

'I want a doctor. I'm going to fetch Dr Ransome!'

Oh no you don't, Maudie thought. She smiled sweetly at him. 'I want you to sit down beside the bed and hold your wife's hand for a few minutes, Mr Stokes.'

'Why? What's happening? What are you going to do?'

'I'm going to pop outside for a moment. I'll be back in no time. Don't you worry about a thing!'

She ran next door and rang the bell urgently. The door was opened at once by a pleasant-faced older woman wearing a wrap-around overall, who greeted Maudie with a smile.

'Can I help you, Nurse?'

'Is your husband home?'

'I'm a widow, as it happens, but my son is here, if that's any help.'

'Can you get him to take Derek Stokes down to the Royal Oak, and keep him there until he's sent for? I can't be doing with having him under my feet all evening. Mr Stokes, I mean, not your son!'

'I know what you mean, Nurse. You get back and I'll send Eddie round in a minute. I'm Nellie Cooper, by the way. Would you like me to come over and do what I can? I could hold the girl's hand, at least. I've had six of my own so I know what's what,' she added, as

Maudie hesitated.

Derek Stokes was led off, protesting loudly. 'There, that's taken care of him,' Nellie announced, shutting the door behind him. 'I'll go and put the kettle on, shall I? Seems to me we could do with a brew after all that upset.'

Reassured by the calm presence of the two women, Pamela Stokes settled down to await the birth of her child. She did start up in alarm when the clock downstairs chimed eleven times.

'Where is Derek? Why isn't he here? It's chucking-out time at the pub, so where's he got to?'

Nellie patted her arm. 'Don't you fret, my love. Our Eddie will look after him. If need be he'll take him in next door and tuck him up on the couch.'

'But what's he been doing all this time? Derek hardly ever takes a drink, so I hope he hasn't been overdoing it!'

Nellie winked at Maudie. 'All the better if he has, eh, Nurse? Nothing like sleeping all your cares away, that's what I always say. He'll wake up to find himself a father, and he'll be proud as punch.'

'Your Eddie is a gem,' Maudie told her.

'He is that, though I say it as shouldn't. And don't you worry, Nurse; he'll see you home when all this is over, if you're not too proud to ride in a van that's had sheep in it.'

'Sheep or not, I'll be more than thankful,' Maudie said. The Llandyfan taxi was never available between the hours of midnight and six o'clock in the morning, and she didn't fancy walking the three miles home without so much as a pocket torch to light her way.

'That's settled, then. And have no fear, Nurse! I can stay here all night and have a kip in this chair after you've gone, so this girl here won't be left alone.'

That was one good thing about people in country places, Maudie thought. They were always willing to pitch in and help each other when necessary. She would miss all that when she married Dick and moved with him to some unknown town. There wasn't time to dwell on that now. Mrs Stokes gasped and cried out in dismay, and further examination showed that the second stage of labour had begun.

At three o'clock in the morning Baby Girl Stokes was ushered into the world, squalling loudly. Maudie laid the child on her mother's tummy while Mrs Stokes cried tears of joy.

'Where is Derek? Why isn't he here? I want to show him the baby!'

'We're not quite finished here yet,' Maudie told her, 'but it won't be long now.'

'I'll just go and find a bucket for the you-know-what,' Nellie said. 'And then I'll run next door and see what's going on.'

'You've been so kind, Mrs Cooper,' Mrs Stokes remarked. 'I think I'd like to call the baby Ellen after you, if that's all right.'

Nellie beamed. 'Delighted, I'm sure!'

Maudie felt a small pang of jealousy, quickly suppressed. She'd had a number of babies named after her, or rather her middle name, Grace. Why shouldn't someone else get a look-in? Nellie's motherly presence had done much to reassure the frightened girl, enabling Maudie to get on with her job. And having a sympathetic older woman next door would be a bonus while the young couple adjusted to the demands of parenthood.

Given last night's performance Derek Stokes was probably going to be like a cat on hot bricks every time the baby cried, or vomited, or filled her nappy with that peculiar yellow mess that newborns ejected. Maudie could imagine him rushing out to summon Dr Ransome. Well, let him get on with it! It was no skin off her nose, as Mrs Hatch was fond of saying, to show she didn't care what people thought.

28

Maudie received a letter from the War Office. It was brief and to the point. The writer thanked her for her esteemed enquiry but they regretted that regulations did not permit them to respond to her query. Information in service records dealing with deceased men and women could not be shared with anyone other than their next of kin. The writer was hers obediently, J Somebody-or-other. Maudie could not decipher the scrawl, but the typed name below the signature read J. Quackenbush.

'Well thank you very much for nothing, Mr Quackenbush, whoever you are!' Maudie muttered. What a waste of a stamp that was! And how did they know that she was not Julian Ransome's next of kin? She might have been a sister, or a cousin. Not every man who went to war had left a wife behind, or had parents living.

On the other hand this must mean that he really was dead, or at least listed as such in their records. Yet had they bothered to check the record at all before shooting off that curt letter?

Maudie had long since decided that war made little tin gods out of quite ordinary people who suddenly found themselves in positions of power. J. Quackenbush might be one such man, getting satisfaction out of putting people in their place.

The second post brought the return of her letter to the Ransomes in Godalming. Somebody had written on it in red ink, 'addressee unknown: return to sender'. Maudie cursed. Well, there was nothing else for it. She would have to telephone Sister Martin.

She knew better than to interrupt the work of Male Surgical with personal business, so it was with great impatience that she waited until late in the evening before contacting her former colleague at home.

'I'm sorry to bother you, Perry,' she began, deliberately using the woman's maiden name in an effort to make her identify with Maudie. As student nurses they had shared many trials and tribulations as they learned their craft, an experience that should have bonded them for life.

'Didn't you get my letter, Rouse?'

'Oh yes, I did, thank you. But there's something else I need to ask now.'

'Go on.'

'Well, Bob mentioned a medical orderly in the page you sent.'

'Did he?'

'Yes. He said that he told you something about him before, in connection with Julian Ransome. Can you recall what it may have been?'

'Funnily enough, I can. This man, whose name I certainly don't remember, was what Bob called the spitting image of Julian. Apparently there was a lot of joshing about it; people asking them if they were twins separated at birth, that sort of thing.'

'And were they? Separated at birth, I mean?'

'Not that I know of. Mind you, I never

did meet the other chap because Bob only ran into him in North Africa, you know. And Bob only told me about it as an interesting fact, seeing that I knew Julian in the old days.'

'Well, well!' Maudie said.

Doris sniffed. 'Mind you, I think they were probably exaggerating. Maybe they did resemble each other a bit, but I'm sure there must have been various differences, like hair colour, for example, or their height.'

'Hmm.'

'Where are you going with all this, Rouse? I know you were sweet on Julian once but that was years ago. You've found somebody else now, so why not leave the handsome doctor firmly in the past, where he belongs?'

Maudie couldn't think of a good answer. 'Oops, sorry, somebody at the door!' she muttered. 'I'll have to go. I'm probably being summoned to a case!' She hung up the phone, gasping slightly.

So Julian Ransome had met a double while serving in North Africa. Not another doctor, to be sure, but a medical orderly, working in a job that was in the same field of endeavour. What if — ? A confused jumble of thoughts swirled around in Maudie's head.

Sitting down, she put her elbows on the kitchen table, resting her head in her hands. This was the information she had hoped for, but now that it had come she was almost overwhelmed by it.

Could it be possible? She wished desperately that Dick was here. She needed to sort out her thoughts before deciding how she should deal with the knowledge she had gained.

Suppose it was true that Julian Ransome had been killed in North Africa, blown up by a land mine. Could the orderly somehow have assumed his identity? And what then? After being demobbed he would have had to establish himself using Julian's credentials, but how? And when that was done, he would have to set himself up in general practice, as Llandyfan's new doctor had done.

Maudie shook her head. This sort of thing was all very well in books, but this was real life. And yet, so much could go wrong in the confusion and chaos of war. Every day the newspapers were full of the most incredible stories. Various people who'd been pronounced dead suddenly reappeared, to general rejoicing. Family members who had been separated found each other again. Missing goods were mysteriously restored to their owners.

'Let's pretend that Dr Ransome is that former orderly,' Maudie murmured, ticking off points on her fingers. Orderlies might be quite well trained, and they certainly must have picked up a lot of expert knowledge serving in the theatre of war. But would any of them know enough to be able to pass themselves off as doctors?

She thought over what she had seen of Dr Ransome in action. Not a lot, really, when it came to male patients, although she had acted as chaperone whenever he needed to examine women. And perhaps that was the real test, for attending to wounded men was hardly likely to have prepared him for dealing with female complaints.

He had sensibly referred several people

to the hospital for tests. He had sent a woman to see his partner, Dr Dean at Midvale, saying that he wanted a second opinion. It had all seemed very right and proper, and his kindly manner seemed to impress the patients favourably. Of course, Maudie wasn't at the surgery every day so she might have missed something, but there had been no complaints against the doctor that she knew of. Had there been any she would certainly have heard about it as she went about her rounds. And according to Mrs Blunt, Cora Beasley had actually said she was delighted with the way things were working out, especially after the debacle of the year before.

All that aside, Maudie was becoming more and more convinced that her crazy theories were right. The Julian Ransome she had known was dead and gone, and his double, or doppelganger, or whatever you liked to call it, was here in Llandyfan masquerading as somebody he was not.

The question was, what was she supposed to do about it? She was quite sure that it was a criminal offence for a layperson to set up in practice as a medical doctor. And she herself might be charged with aiding and abetting a criminal if she neglected to report the crime. But more than that, the patients could suffer harm from being treated by an unqualified person. And that, in her eyes, was an even worse crime. She knew she had to act, and soon. Sadly, she rather liked the man — or could that be because she had once loved the original Julian Ransome?

She supposed she should go and speak to the police, perhaps that inspector who had come to reassure Mr Blunt about his safety. But the thought of trying to explain her theories to him made her squirm. As she knew from what Dick had told her that the police often received tips from well-meaning people who had got hold of the wrong end of the stick and so managed to waste police time. In criminal cases every lead had to be explored, but being led in the wrong direction was most annoying.

Then there were those who were just wrong-headed or loopy, and Maudie certainly didn't want to be bracketed with people like that!

She could just imagine the look on the inspector's face when she unfolded a tale involving men blown to death in Africa, mistaken identity, obtaining jobs by fraud, and all the rest. And when it came out, as it surely must, that a Dr Julian Ransome had jilted Maudie, that would put the kibosh on it, well and truly! They would decide that she was out to get her revenge. Dick's colleagues would feel sorry for him having to marry a hysterical woman such as Maudie Rouse, and it might even spoil his job chances further down the line.

Her other option was to write to the British Medical Council, who were better equipped to deal with matters like this. Their job was to regulate the profession and, in extreme cases, to have the offender struck off the medical register, rendering him or her unable to practice.

Yes, that was the way to go. And if they investigated the doctor and discovered some rational explanation for all this, and Maudie was mistaken, the business could be settled quietly, behind the scenes. By contrast, if she approached the police the *Midvale Chronicle* would get wind of it, and there would be a great uproar. She could see the headlines now: 'Scandal hits doctor's surgery again! Llandyfan patients duped by fraudulent medic!'

She made up her mind that she would lie low for a couple of days, to reassure herself that she was doing the right thing. Then she would act.

29

Mrs Blunt called across the street to Maudie. 'Hello, Nurse. We've had some news. Would you care to drop in for tea today, say about three o'clock, if you're free?'

'Right ho! Thank you very much.' She was glad of the opportunity, for perhaps now she'd be able to pin the vicar down to a definite date for her wedding. She was expecting to see Dick at the weekend and it would be good to have something definite to tell him. She was uncomfortably aware that she'd shot down too many of his suggestions recently, and she didn't want him getting the idea that she was lukewarm about their union.

She had to do something about her wedding cake, too. Fruitcake needs time to mature, preferably wrapped in a piece of butter muslin soaked in sherry. And after that it has to be covered in a layer of marzipan before the royal icing is put on.

Neither she nor Dick had any close relatives living within easy reach, and as they were keeping the wedding small it seemed foolish to invite distant cousins who lived far away. Better by far to send them an announcement of the nuptials, accompanied by a sliver of cake in a tiny cardboard box.

Maudie's day went smoothly as she went about her home visits. All the new arrivals seemed to be thriving, although little Ellen Stokes seemed to be developing nappy rash.

'I don't understand it,' her mother said. 'I try to change her as soon as she wets herself but I can't go and feel her nappy every five minutes to see if it's soaked.'

'Do try not to worry,' Maudie told her. 'Nobody ever died from nappy rash, or at least, I've never heard of it.'

She regretted her cheerful words as soon as they were out of her mouth. Mrs Stokes stared at her in horror. 'Do you mean it's that serious, Nurse? What shall I do? Must I take her to the doctor?'

'Calm down, I was only joking,'

Maudie told her. 'I'll give you a tube of zinc cream to be going on with, and that should help. When the warm weather comes, let little Ellen lie outside on a blanket without a nappy on, to let the sun get at her bottom. Not too long, mind; we don't want her getting sunburned.' Fat chance of that in Britain, she thought, remembering so many past summers when plans had been spoiled by wet weather.

'I didn't realise that bringing up a baby was so complicated, Nurse. What with all the broken nights she gives us I hardly know if I'm coming or going.'

'She'll soon start sleeping through the night,' Maudie advised. 'In the meantime, do try to have a little lie-down in the afternoons. Don't be afraid to let the housework slide. Giving birth is a major event in a woman's life. It takes time to recover properly.'

Maudie found Marie Jukes placidly folding clean laundry, while a tow-headed toddler played at her feet. The woman was expecting baby number six any day now, and with her rosy cheeks and contented smile, she appeared to be blooming.

'I think this is a football in here, not a baby!' she told Maudie, patting her bulging abdomen. 'Do you think this is twins, Nurse?'

'I'm pretty sure it's just the one, Mrs Jukes,' Maudie told her, laughing. 'I admit you're a bit bigger this time, but you have had five children. Your muscles must have stretched a bit. Mind you, you do look ready to pop! Be sure to send for me as soon as you feel the first twinge of pain. I've a feeling in my bones that you may be in for a short labour this time.'

'The shorter the better, as far as I'm concerned, Nurse.' She picked up a sheet from the huge pile of dry washing in the basket. Maudie took hold of the other end and helped her to fold it. She looked back with nostalgia at her days in hospital, when nurses had made beds working two by two in unison. Nowadays she usually worked without help, and bed-making meant a lot of leaning over, or walking from one side to the other.

'Go potty!' the toddler announced,

dancing from one foot to the other. His mother leaned over and felt his little trousers.

'Too late, I'm afraid! Take them off, my love, and we'll find you a dry pair in a minute.' She rummaged through the basket of garments. 'I know I washed a couple of pairs yesterday. They must be in here somewhere.'

Maudie plunged her hands into the pile and came up with a pair of red corduroy dungarees.

'How about these?'

'No, those belong to Mark, my five-year-old. Paul would be swamped in those. Ah, here's what I was looking for.' She held up a patched and faded pair of shorts, obviously a hand-me-down. Probably young Paul had never had a new item of clothing in his life, and these shorts would no doubt be passed on to the new arrival in due course. Maudie accepted the garment and expertly changed the tiny boy, while his mother continued her work of folding the family laundry.

'When are you getting married, Nurse?

It must be any day now?'

'Some time in July, Mrs Jukes. I'm seeing the vicar today to pin down the date.'

'Be sure to give us plenty of warning, Nurse! There's a few of us who will want to see you coming out of church in all your finery. I do love a wedding, don't you?'

Even when it leads to six children? Maudie thought. Well, Mrs Jukes seemed happy enough with her lot, and that was all that mattered.

'And how is your hubby-to-be? Looking forward to the great day, is he?'

'He's anxiously awaiting the results of his exams, to see if he'll be promoted to sergeant,' Maudie said proudly.

'Sergeant, eh? We'll have to mind our Ps and Qs round here then, won't we, Nurse?'

Maudie smiled. This was not the time to explain that Dick might well be posted elsewhere, in which case she, too, would be moving away from the area. She knew that women came to depend on their midwife for advice and support long after their children had come into the world. While another midwife would be assigned to the district after she was gone, she liked to think that she might be missed. At least, she hoped that would be the case. She felt a great affinity with Llandyfan and its people and it would be a wrench to leave.

Maudie arrived at the vicarage right on time. Her day had gone well and she was able to stop in at her cottage for a refreshing bath before going out to tea. Then, comfortably clad in an aertex shirt, a blue cotton skirt and Clark's sandals, she strolled down the road to see her friend.

'Hello, Nurse. Do come in. Tea will be ready in a minute. I meant to serve it in the garden but the wasps are too bad out there, so we'll have to eat in the drawing room instead.'

'My granny used to trap wasps in a jam jar,' Maudie said.

'So did mine. She used to use a jar with a little jam remaining in it, half-filled with water. Ugh! It works all right but then you have to clean out the jar afterwards, and I can't bear that! Never mind, we'll be indoors where they can't get at us.'

'You said you have something to tell me,' Maudie prompted.

'Yes, but we'll wait for Harold, if you don't mind. He'll be here presently and it's his news, really. Now, I hope you're hungry! I've made cucumber sandwiches and marmite sandwiches, and an apple tart.'

'Lovely!'

'I was going to make a sponge cake as well, but I had a string of interruptions all morning. People wanting to discuss the Scouts' jumble sale, the Mothers' Union sale of work and the restoration of the church kneelers. They all seem to involve me in some way, but it doesn't leave me much time to myself.'

When at last the vicar arrived, he came to the point at once, fortunately for Maudie's blood pressure. 'We've heard from that inspector again,' he said. 'It's all been a case of mistaken identity.'

Maudie's jaw dropped open. For one startled moment she thought he was talking about Julian Ransome.

'Yes,' Mrs Blunt chimed in, 'the vicar who served on that tribunal was a Reverend Howard Blunt, not Harold, of course.'

'But how did the mix-up happen?'

'Apparently the other Mr Blunt — the one that Marsh was thinking about — passed away shortly after the war,' the vicar said. 'When Marsh was planning his campaign of terror he searched the church directories and I was the only H. Blunt he found. Mind you, this Howard wouldn't have been listed among the Anglicans in any case. I'm told he was a Presbyterian minister.'

'So all this was never anything to do with you at all,' Maudie said. 'That must be a relief.'

'Except that if Mr Marsh had carried on with his campaign and it finally led to violence, it wouldn't have mattered whether Harold was the one he was looking for or not, would it?'

'A Harold by any other name would smell as sweet,' the vicar said, misquoting Shakespeare. His wife looked at him over the top of her glasses. 'Well, perhaps not,' he finished lamely.

Mrs Blunt heaved a sigh. 'Harold has written to that poor man, explaining the mix-up and expressing sympathy for the loss of his son.'

'Very Christian of him, I'm sure,' Maudie said.

The vicar looked at her rather sternly. 'That is the nature of my calling, Nurse. I do strive to live up to that, you know.' Now it was Maudie's turn to look abashed.

Mrs Blunt, that veteran of a thousand minor parish crises, hastened to lighten the atmosphere. 'Tea is all ready,' she announced. 'Shall we go through?'

30

By the time Maudie returned to her cottage, may of the details of her wedding had been settled. The vicar had given her a firm booking for the third Saturday in July, pending confirmation from Dick that he'd be able to get the time off.

'Just in case that isn't possible, Nurse, the second and fourth Saturdays are still open, but I hope you can confirm soon. June is already booked up completely, and in fact I have more than one wedding to perform on two of those Saturdays. I expect that those who have left it too late, like the foolish virgins in the New Testament, will be rushing to book in July instead.'

Of course the said virgins hadn't been trying to firm up their wedding arrangements, even though a wedding was involved in Christ's parable, recorded in St Matthew's gospel, but Maudie knew what he meant.

263

When the vicar had gone, she and Mrs Blunt got down to other important details, such as the wedding cake. 'I thought I'd go into Midvale and speak to the woman at the bakery,' Maudie said.

'Well, I must admit they do a very elegant-looking cake,' Mrs Blunt said, 'but the last time I tasted one I thought it was rather dry. Now little Mrs Groves at Hilltop Farm does a very nice fruitcake as a sideline, and she's a dab hand at icing and decorating, too. Why not ask her to make it? It will save you some money and do her a good turn at the same time. I believe she even has tiny figurines of a bride and groom to put on top of the cake. Those are only on loan of course. You'd have to return them after the reception.'

'Mm.'

'Have you given any thought to where you'll live after you're married, Nurse? I can still remember how excited I was, planning our first home. Of course we didn't have much choice because Harold was assigned to a parish by the bishop. It wasn't as if we could go out and choose where we wanted to settle.'

'It's the same with us,' Maudie said. 'It all depends on where Dick is sent. I imagine he's at liberty to turn down a posting, but he mustn't rock the boat too much if he wants to get on in the force.'

'Perhaps they'll keep him on at Midvale. That would be nice.'

Maudie wrinkled her nose, thinking over what her friend had said. 'A lot depends on whether he passes his sergeant's exams. They already have a sergeant there and I doubt they'd want two in one small station. Even if Dick has failed his exam — heaven forbid — and they let him stay on as a beat constable, we couldn't possibly live in his bachelor flat. There's barely enough room for one person, let alone two.'

'And how is he getting along at Hendon? Does he think he'll be transferred to the detective side when his training there is over?'

Maudie sighed. 'I simply don't know. That's all Greek to me, I'm afraid. If he does pass his sergeant's exams and he gets the promotion, and then he does well enough in his courses at the police college, what will come of that? I rather doubt they'd make him a detective sergeant right away. I liken it to my own experience. When I became state registered I felt I'd made it to the top; I'd endured my training and become qualified in my profession. But then I went in for my midder and once again I was at the bottom of the heap, a quivering mass of jelly when I did my first delivery under supervision.'

'Oh, I'm sure it couldn't have been that bad,' Mrs Blunt said, laughing.

'You have no idea! But this causes me concern when I think about what lies ahead for Dick, you see. Wouldn't he have to start at the bottom again, as a detective constable? But if so, then what was the point of all that studying for the sergeant's exams?'

'What will be, will be, Nurse. If all else fails you can always have a room here with us for a while. These places were built in the days when the clergy had huge families, and we have six unused bedrooms upstairs.'

'That is such a kind offer,' Maudie murmured, and she meant it. But at the same time she had no intention of starting her married life in the home of the local vicar. Something else would turn up. It had to!

* * *

Dick came home on leave that weekend. Having heard the chugging sound of his approaching motorcycle, Maudie rushed into the street, not caring who saw her. He was dismounting when she flung her arms around his neck.

'Here, steady on, you'll have me over,' Dick mumbled, looking pleased all the same.

'Come on in! I've got so much to tell you.'

'So have I,' he said, removing his leather helmet and goggles and smoothing down his ruffled hair.

'I've missed you so much,' she told him, hanging onto his arm as they made their way into the house.

'Same here, old girl! Never mind, it

won't be long until we're man and wife. Speaking of which, what's the news on that front? Have you been to see the vicar?'

'We're booked in for the third Saturday in July, if you can get the time off. I mean, it's not just the Saturday, is it? We need a few days for our honeymoon as well.'

'I'll look into it as soon as I get back. What are our options if I can't manage that date?' Maudie told him. 'Right, then. I'll get onto it right away and I'll give you a ring to let you know. What else is new?'

Maudie told him about her plans for the reception, not forgetting the wedding cake. 'I've picked out my dress, too, in Fab Fashions, that upmarket ladies' dress shop in Midvale, and I've put down a deposit on it. I'll be able to pick it up when I get paid at the end of the month.'

'Should I go in and have a look at it?'

'No!' Maudie shrieked. 'It's unlucky for the groom to see the dress before the big day.'

'That's only if the bride is wearing it. What will you be wearing on your head?'

'I haven't decided that yet. What is more to the point, what will you be wearing?'

'It's a toss-up between my uniform or my demob suit.'

'Not that awful demob suit!' The suits that were issued to men on leaving the services were famous for their dreadful appearance, being poorly cut from material that nobody in his right mind would appreciate.

'I think you should have a nice new suit made,' she told him. 'Dark grey, perhaps, or possibly a nice pinstripe.'

'Wouldn't that be a bit of a waste for just one day, old girl? I'd gallop down the aisle in it and after that it would hang in the back of my wardrobe for years, gathering moths.'

'Dick Bryant! You'd get plenty of wear out of it! We'll have other weddings to go to, and formal occasions galore. Besides, when you switch to the detective side you won't be in uniform then. You'll have to wear mufti, won't you?'

This set him off in an excited account of all that he'd seen and done and learned while he was at Hendon.

'The great Tom Barrett himself came to give us a lecture on the scientific methods used in modern police work!' he enthused.

'Who is Tom Barrett when he's at home?' she asked, earning herself an incredulous stare.

'Detective Chief Superintendant Thomas Barrett!' he said. 'Surely you've heard of Barrett of the Yard? He's one of the Big Five.'

'Fancy!'

Dick was well launched on his story now. 'Surely you've heard of him, Maudie. He's headed up the Scotland Yard team that have solved some of the most famous crimes since the war. Don't you remember the Neville Heath murders? The case was splashed all over the *News of the World*.'

Maudie nodded. Who could forget the former RAF flying ace who had lured two unfortunate women to their deaths in 1946? And no doubt she had read about other important cases dealt with by Scotland Yard. But as for the men who had investigated those crimes, she knew no more about them than the man in the moon, and why should she? If they had been famous surgeons she might have been on firmer ground. To each person his own trade, she thought.

31

Maudie viewed the week ahead with some misgivings. She had hoped to discuss with Dick her problem with Julian Ransome, but he had been so full of excitement about his new experiences that she hadn't wanted to dampen his enthusiasm. And of course she was interested in what he had to say, as any good wife-to-be should be.

Looking at the calendar in her little office, she decided that she must pop in to see Marie Jukes today. While the woman was an old hand at childbirth, Maudie wanted her to take no chances. If the baby should come too quickly, without Maudie's skill to slow down the delivery, the patient's tissues might tear, and that must be avoided at all costs.

Then she heard footsteps approaching as someone entered the main door of the parish hall. By the heavy tread she surmised it to be a man, but the lack of haste ruled out Marie Jukes's husband, coming to summon her to his wife's bedside. It must be the vicar then, or the sexton, perhaps. That most likely meant that it was nothing to do with her, and she could get on with her day as planned.

'Good morning, Nurse.' Maudie's head came up in a hurry. Somehow she managed to summon up a smile.

'Hello, Dr Ransome. What brings you here?'

'I think you and I need to have a little talk,' he replied.

'Oh, yes? Is it about the schedule at the surgery?'

He picked up the chair that she kept for visitors and placed it squarely in the doorway. He sat down. Now there was no way that Maudie could get past him. Her way of escape was completely blocked off. Her office had been made by partitioning off a corner of the parish hall: there was only one door leading into it, and no window.

'I think you know very well what all this is about, Nurse Rouse.'

'Sorry, I don't know what you mean,'

Maudie said, stalling for time.

'Then perhaps I should tell you that I've had a phone call from a certain Sister Martin at your old hospital.'

'Oh,' said Maudie.

'Oh, indeed! The good lady congratulated me on having survived the war. It appears that she'd heard I was dead and she remembered me from her training days at Mary and Martha's, where she still works. But of course she wasn't only calling for that reason. She so kindly wanted to let me know that a certain Nurse Maudie Rouse wanted to invite me to her upcoming wedding. Apparently you and I were an item before the war, Nurse! I must say I was rather surprised to hear about that.'

Maudie said nothing to this, for what was there to say? She only knew that she had to get past him somehow, out of this trap and out of his clutches.

Where are you when I need you, Mr Jukes? But all was quiet. Once before, she had been saved from a murderer by the timely arrival of an expectant father, but it seemed that she was out of luck this time around. Nobody came.

'What puzzles me, Nurse, is why you didn't say anything when we first met at the reception given by Mrs Beasley. Wouldn't it have been natural for you to say that we already knew each other? Or did you realise right away that I wasn't the Julian Ransome you used to know?'

'I was shocked, that was all. You had treated me pretty badly before the war, and when you more or less ignored me at the reception I thought it was just you being arrogant again. Sending the message that I was beneath your notice.'

'So when did you begin to suspect that I'm not Julian Ransome?'

'I didn't! I mean, who are you then?'

'Really, Nurse! I hope you never go on the stage. You're a poor excuse for an actress, you know. Your friend Sister Martin has told you my story, hasn't she? It was just bad luck that her husband happened to meet me with the real Julian Ransome in North Africa, and wrote to his wife about it. Even worse luck that the woman has kept his letters. Even so, I might have got away with it if Little Miss

Snoopy hadn't come along to spoil things! I suppose you've told that policeman boyfriend of yours all about it, haven't you?'

'I haven't told anybody,' Maudie said, hoping to defuse the situation so that he would go away and leave her alone. She realised her mistake at once.

'Well now, that is good news. You do realise that I can't let you live to tell the tale, Nurse Rouse? I promise you that you won't feel much. One little squeeze around the neck and it will be all over.'

Maudie's gaze went to a kidney basin on her desk, half hidden by a pile of unfinished paperwork. A mother had popped in earlier, bringing with her a small boy for his immunization jab. He had been absent from school when the other children had received theirs and it was important that he should receive the protection it offered.

The needle, which was usually disposed of carefully in a screw-topped jar, had been forgotten by Maudie. Still attached to its small glass syringe, it was now lying in the dish. Its presence there gave

Maudie one small shred of hope. If Ransome came for her with murderous intent she would try to make a lunge for the syringe and jab him with it before he could throttle her.

But what part of his anatomy should she go for? Such a tiny needle would barely penetrate his clothing, let alone stop him in his tracks. She would have to aim for his eye. He was taller than she was, but she'd played netball in her day, and she could still leap with the best of them. But could she possibly bring herself to stab a man in the eyeball? She shuddered at the thought.

'What's the matter, Nurse? Feeling a little worried, are we? Why don't you let the nice doctor take care of you now? All your troubles will soon be over and you can have a nice long rest.'

Anger stirred in Maudie's breast. *You don't play cat and mouse with me, Julian Ransome, or whatever your name is,* she told herself. She wasn't going to go quietly! Where was the spirit that had got them through Dunkirk? She would struggle. Scream. Claw his face. She might not succeed in saving her own life, but she would jolly well leave as many clues as possible so that he'd be brought to justice sooner or later.

Keep him talking, she told herself. *It's just possible that somebody may come.* She took a deep breath.

'If you're going to kill me you might just as well tell me the whole story,' she said. 'I'd really hate to die not knowing. I really admire what you've done, you know. It must have taken a great deal of intelligence to take the place of a doctor like Julian Ransome and I'd love to know how you managed it.'

Dick had told her that criminals were often caught out because of their own vanity. They needed to boast about their achievements, to have people admire them for their cleverness. Arsonists were a case in point. Whenever a fire was set the police and firemen surveyed the onlookers carefully, for ten to one the chap would be there among the crowd, gloating.

Now, if she could appeal to this man's vanity, it would buy her some time.

The false Dr Ransome looked at her steadily. 'I suppose it wouldn't hurt, for all the good it may do you. I have all the time in the world, even if you do not!'

Please, Lord, please send somebody to get me out of this, she prayed. The idea of never seeing Dick again filled her with terrible grief. This was followed by the silly thought that she wouldn't get to wear her lovely rose-pink dress now. If the worst-case scenario came about she hoped they'd bury her in it.

'When did you first find out that you had a double?' she asked.

'Not until I was shipped to North Africa. I was working in a field hospital one day when a nurse addressed me as Dr Ransome, telling me I was wanted immediately in theatre. I had quite a time convincing her that I wasn't the man she wanted. She got quite annoyed with me, saying I mustn't play stupid games when a man's life could be at stake.'

'And how did you make her believe you?'

'A few minutes later Julian Ransome came striding round the corner and stopped in front of us. You should have seen the look on her face! And Ransome was pretty taken aback too. There wasn't time to stand around talking right then, but he called back to me over his shoulder, saying that we must get together for a drink. It was such an incredible coincidence that after that we became quite good friends. Oh, I know that in civilian life a doctor and an orderly would hardly have mingled in the same circles, but war often makes a difference, don't you think?'

32

Maudie felt an urgent need to go to the loo. She told herself that she mustn't give in to the idea. If she asked Ransome to let her use the toilet he would probably interpret that as a ruse to get away, if only by locking herself in. Then he might kill her without stopping to think about it.

'Just what is your real name, anyway?' she demanded. 'Don't tell me that it really is Ransome? That would be too much of a coincidence.'

'Ian Daly,' he said. 'There's no harm in your knowing that now, I suppose.'

'And is it really 'Doctor', or only 'Mister'?'

He shrugged. 'Just plain 'Mister', I'm afraid. I do have a good science degree, and before the war I was admitted to medical school on the strength of that. I'd just completed my first year when war broke out, and pretty soon after that I was called up.'

'But doctors were badly needed. Couldn't you have applied to go on with your training? After all, nobody knew how long the war would last, and you might have been of more use with some qualifications.'

'Don't think that didn't occur to me! But I was pressed into service just the same, and the army in its wisdom had me transformed into an orderly.'

Daly was quiet for a while. The clock on the wall ticked loudly into the silence. He had sounded bitter. But then war had a habit of destroying the best-laid plans of mice and men, as Robert Burns might have put it. Now she understood how this man had been able to masquerade as a doctor in England. His pre-war training had equipped him with a little knowledge and he'd had first-hand experience of how the system worked.

'What happened when Julian Ransome was killed?' she asked. Daly, who seemed to have been looking at something a long way off, came to with a start, focussing on Maudie as if surprised to find her still there.

'Oh, well we were travelling in a convoy: a lot of us, in a variety of different vehicles. Julian was in the cab of a lorry near the front of the group and I was in the back of one about fifty yards to the rear. Suddenly there was this explosion and all hell broke loose. I was pitched out of our lorry and I knew no more until I woke up in hospital. I later heard a lot of different versions of events. Some said we were misdirected into a minefield; others thought we'd been ambushed in some way. The top brass interviewed me about it but I was really no help at all. It was all just a blur.'

Maudie tried to picture the whole sorry scene, one that must have been repeated many times and in many places during the war. She decided that she was grateful to that starchy woman from Queen Alexandra's Nursing Corps who had told her to stay in England and deliver more little soldiers for future wars. Midwifery certainly involved bloodshed and pain, but she had yet to see anybody blown to pieces in front of her eyes.

'Then people started calling me Captain Ransome. They said they wanted to get me better as soon as possible because my services were badly needed. I did tell them once or twice that I was Ian Daly, but nobody took any notice. I had some head injuries and they must have thought I was rambling, I suppose.

'One day a chap came in and told me I was being sent home. 'You've got a Blighty one, you lucky devil. I wouldn't mind getting blown up if it would earn me a ticket out of this mess!' So the next thing I knew I was in a convalescent home in Berkshire, with people still calling me Dr Ransome.'

'So was that when you came up with the idea of adopting his identity?' Maudie wondered.

'It came to me in the middle of one night when I couldn't sleep. We'd had a useless sort of doctor coming in to see the chaps on the ward, and if it hadn't been for a nursing sister who covered up his mistakes a lot of us would have been in trouble. He didn't seem to have much idea of the right dosage of some of the stuff he prescribed. I know she made adjustments there. Of course, had she been found out she'd have been dismissed instantly, never allowed to practise again, and would probably have been slapped into prison too.

'Well, I thought about that idiot doctor, and I said to myself that I could do his job just as well, or better, and that wasn't just vanity, Nurse Rouse! And that's when it came to me. Why not do Ransome's job? I'd come to know him pretty well and I'd found out a lot about his background. I knew I could carry it off if I happened to come across anyone who'd heard of him before. That was until I met you, Nurse Nosy Parker Rouse!

'I didn't look on it as doing anything really wrong. In fact, I was just continuing his work where he left off. Carrying the torch, so to speak. And where was the harm in that?'

'I'm sure I don't know, Mr Daly.' Maudie decided that what he had done was very wrong indeed, but she wasn't going to tell him that. Upsetting the man might be her passport to the next world!

And what a strange existence it was, where mere coincidence should send the two men to the same place, there to begin a chain of lies and deceit, and a second coincidence would deliver Ian Daly into the hands of Julian Ransome's former girlfriend. Nemesis, thy name is Maudie Rouse.

'Why did you do it, Mr Daly?' she asked now. 'You were so far along your career path before the war, why didn't you just return to medical school now? I believe that the government has schemes to help returning veterans continue their education.'

'Pooh! More red tape! No, Nurse. I consider I have quite enough medical knowledge to enable me to work in a place like Llandyfan. It's not as if I set myself up to be a brain specialist or the like. In general practice in a rural area one doesn't see much beyond the basics. Any serious cases get treated in hospital, and well you know it. Years ago doctors depended on their diagnostic skills alone, whereas today we have access to all sorts of tests that help the medical profession arrive at a plan of treatment.'

Maudie had had enough of this. 'Look here, Mr Daly, why don't you leave right now? I promise I'll give you a head start before I tell anyone about this. You've done wrong but at least they can't hang you for it. You haven't killed anybody while you've been here, after all.' *And I hope I shan't be first on the list,* she thought, but she couldn't wait around any longer. The little Jukes boy wasn't the only one who needed to go potty!

Female voices alerted them to the arrival of visitors to the parish hall. With mounting hope Maudie recognised Cora Beasley, who was president of the Mothers' Union and the owner of the doctor's surgery. The other arrival was the sexton's wife.

Maudie stood up quickly. She was pretty sure that Ian Daly wasn't carrying a gun, and he could hardly manage to strangle all three of them at once.

'Yoo-hoo, Mrs Beasley!' she called. 'Can I have a word?'

Mrs Beasley started to come forward

but stopped when she recognised Maudie's visitor.

'I am so sorry, Dr Ransome! I didn't mean to interrupt your consultation. I'll see you later, Nurse.'

But Daly leapt to his feet and rushed towards the door, elbowing the two ladies aside in his flight for freedom.

'Well, really!' Mrs Beasley said.

Maudie burst into tears. The two ladies looked at her in concern.

'Dear me, Nurse, whatever is the matter?'

'He didn't try to, er, interfere with you, did he?' the sexton's wife asked in a shocked whisper.

'Yes, he did!' Maudie bawled, as she bolted towards the door of the ladies' cloakroom. That wasn't exactly what the woman had meant, but Daly had certainly meant to do Maudie a mischief. At least, that was what he had led her to believe.

33

'And that's the whole story,' Maudie concluded when Cora Beasley had escorted her to the vicarage, with the sexton's wife bringing up the rear.

The vicar stared at her in consternation, while his wife bustled round filling up hot-water bottles and producing hot, sweet tea. 'I don't know what this world is coming to, really I don't,' he said. 'So much evil everywhere. And poor Nurse always seems to find herself right in the middle of it. Well, all I can say is, I am glad that you'll soon be married, Nurse, with a good husband to take care of you.'

Maudie muttered something rude under her breath. She heard a soft voice say into her ear, 'I know! Sometimes he affects me like that, too!'

She looked up into the smiling face of her friend, Joan Blunt, who was holding out a mug of scalding tea. 'You drink this, Nurse. Just what the doctor ordered!'

Now it was Mrs Blunt's turn to blush. 'Or not, as the case may be,' she muttered.

'I don't know why these things always have to happen to me!' Cora Beasley stated loudly. 'Out of the goodness of my heart I turn my gatehouse into a surgery for the benefit of the people of Llandyfan, and what do I get in return? A murder on my very doorstep, and now a doctor who turns out not to be qualified at all! I feel as though somebody has laid a curse on me. What do they call such goings-on in America? A hex, isn't it? Well somebody has laid one on me. And it's no good you giving me that look, vicar!'

'Oh, but the poor vicar has been vexed too, Mrs Beasley,' piped up the sexton's wife. 'Mowed down in the street, he was, because of some nutter from up London.'

'Hexed, Gladys Pratt. I said hexed, not vexed, although I daresay the poor man is vexed as well, aren't you, Mr Blunt?'

Maudie decided that she couldn't take any more of this. 'I'll be going now,' she said. 'I have to lie down.'

'So I should think,' Gladys said, her sharp features twisted in sympathy. 'Did you hear how that brute treated our nurse, Mr Blunt? He tried to take advantage of her, right there in the parish hall!'

A great wave of laughter swelled up inside Maudie that she felt powerless to control. Suddenly releasing a loud guffaw, she laughed until the tears rolled down her cheeks while Joan Blunt patted her gently on the back.

'Hysterical,' Cora Beasley said. 'Not that I'm surprised, after what happened to her today. I recommend a good dose of castor oil. That should set her right.'

'Everyone is a doctor,' Maudie said, when at last she regained her breath.

★ ★ ★

All in all, Maudie was thankful when Dick returned home for good. 'How has everything been here?' he wanted to know.

'Oh, much the same as usual. We've had no more murders since you were gone, although it was touch and go for a while.'

'Anyone we know?'

'Let's forget about murder and mayhem for a while. Tell me how you've been getting along.'

'Well, I passed my sergeant's exams,' he told her, trying to look modest but not quite succeeding.

Maudie hugged him. 'I always knew you would! What sort of mark did you get?'

'Seventy two per cent overall.'

'Not bad!'

'Actually I was hoping to do rather better, but least I got through, and that counts for something.'

'Have you any idea what happens to you next? Are they giving you a fat new job with lots of extra pay?'

'Nothing yet. I'm hoping that the super is saving that up for a surprise; a sort of extra wedding present. Speaking of weddings, are we all set for the big day?'

'I think so, unless you've forgotten to get yourself a best man.'

'I thought I'd ask Bill Brewer. You know, that constable with the hair that sticks straight up when he removes his helmet.'

'I don't want him looking like a walking lavatory brush at my wedding, and he can't keep his helmet on in church!'

'Don't be so unkind. I'll make him smarm it down with Brylcreem. Will that please your ladyship?'

'Oh, have it your own way,' Maudie told him as she snuggled closer into his arms. Much as she had resented the vicar's suggestion that she needed a husband to protect her, she had to admit that she felt safe with Dick.

She didn't tell him that she'd had difficulty finding a matron of honour for herself. She had meant to enlist a friend from her days at their nurses' training school, only to learn that she had gone to Australia to visit her parents, who had emigrated there as 'ten-pound Poms'. And she certainly wasn't about to invite Sister Martin, despite heavy hints coming from that direction. The silly woman had really dropped her in it with Dr Julian Ransome, or Ian Daly as Maudie now knew him to be.

Joan Blunt had been delighted to accept Maudie's invitation to accompany her down the aisle and had agreed to go shopping with her to help her find a suitable hat. As Maudie said, one that was 'flowery, but not over the top'.

The wedding cake had been completed by Mrs Groves, with the china figurines installed on top. Just how close they had come to leaving the bride off her pedestal was something Maudie intended to keep from Dick until she could find the right moment to tell him.

Meanwhile, the third Saturday in July was fast approaching. Maudie had managed to lose that unwelcome five pounds and she was able to try on the rose-pink silk dress without having to suck in her breath. Dick had invested in a very nice dark grey suit, with a minimum of fuss about the exorbitant price.

As for Dr Julian Ransome, his disappearance had been a nine days' wonder in the village. Gladys Pratt had confused everyone by saying that the doctor had made a pass at Maudie, who had given him his come-uppance by reporting him to the local bobbies, which was as it should be, 'what with her being one of their own now, more or less'.

Asked if this was true, Maudie told Mrs Hatch that the doctor had gone off to join the Foreign Legion.

'I never can tell if that nurse is telling the truth or not,' Mrs Hatch grumbled to a friend, who was examining the Cox's Orange Pippins that sat in a box on the counter. 'The Foreign Legion, indeed! Didn't he get enough of desert sand during the war?'

'Don't ask me,' the friend replied, 'But that's our Maudie. And I, for one, can't wait to see her coming out of the church on the arm of that handsome bobby. You'll be there too, won't you?'

'I suppose so,' Mrs Hatch said, shrugging. 'If she can find a husband at her age there's help for all of us yet!'

THE END

We do hope that you have enjoyed reading this large print book.

Did you know that all of our titles are available for purchase?

We publish a wide range of high quality large print books including:

Romances, Mysteries, Classics
General Fiction
Non Fiction and Westerns

Special interest titles available in large print are:

The Little Oxford Dictionary
Music Book, Song Book
Hymn Book, Service Book

Also available from us courtesy of Oxford University Press:

Young Readers' Dictionary
(large print edition)
Young Readers' Thesaurus
(large print edition)

For further information or a free brochure, please contact us at:
Ulverscroft Large Print Books Ltd.,
The Green, Bradgate Road, Anstey,
Leicester, LE7 7FU, England.
Tel: (00 44) 0116 236 4325
Fax: (00 44) 0116 234 0205

STORM EVIL

John Robb

A terrible storm sweeps across a vast desert of North Africa. Five legionnaires and a captain on a training course are caught in it and take refuge in a ruined temple. Into the temple, too, come four Arabs laden with hate for the Legion captain. Then a beautiful aviator arrives — the estranged wife of the officer. When darkness falls, and the storm rages outside, the Arabs take a slow and terrible vengeance against the captain. Death strikes suddenly, often, and in a grotesque form . . .

ROOKIE COP

Richard A. Lupoff

America, June 1940. Nick Train has given up his dreams of a boxing championship after a brief and unsuccessful career in the ring. When one of his pals takes the examination for the police academy, Nick decides to join him. But what started out as a whim turns into a dangerous challenge, as Nick plays a precarious double game of collector for the mob and mole for a shadowy enforcement body . . . Will the rookie cop's luck hold?